What do the [illegible] look like — [illegible] laid off from [illegible] their son look like etc

SILENT JUSTICE

what did the dead teacher look like.

Rayven T. Hill

Track down the young suspect if you know who he is why do you have to track him down. How do you know he is young.

(no description at all)

Ray of Joy
Publishing

Ray of Joy Publishing
Toronto

detective [illegible] to the end. [illegible]

Books by Rayven T. Hill

Blood and Justice
Cold Justice
Justice for Hire
Captive Justice
Justice Overdue
Justice Returns
Personal Justice
Silent Justice
Web of Justice
Fugitive Justice

Visit rayventhill.com for more information
on these and future releases.

Published by Ray of Joy Publishing
Toronto

ISBN-13: 978-0-9947781-5-4

SILENT JUSTICE

CHAPTER 1

DAY 1 - Monday, 8:49 p.m.

NINA WHITE leaned back in her swivel chair and glanced out the large window in her office. The street, a hub of activity during the day, was now strangely quiet and peaceful. A car drove by slowly, its headlights cutting a narrow path through the gathering darkness. It pulled to the far side of the street a hundred feet away and its lights died. A dark figure sat unmoving in the driver seat.

Nina yawned and turned back to her desk. Although on rare occasions she had worked into the wee hours of the morning, she didn't often work past five p.m. But enrollment at Richmond North High School was growing and her workload grew along with it. She decided it was time to pack it in for the evening and perhaps get some rare time with her patient husband. She could get a fresh start early in the morning.

She glanced out the window again. The driver of the car had disappeared and she craned her neck to see if she could spot him. There were no houses along this street, the school property taking up the whole of one side, a block-long park on the other.

She closed the folder on her desk, stood, and tucked it into a file cabinet. She felt pleased with her day's accomplishments. Lately, her evenings had been spent developing a new guidance curriculum. As school counselor, it was her job and her pleasure to provide students the support they needed to succeed in school and fulfill their dreams. Their dreams were her dreams and she took her job seriously.

Nina retrieved her handbag from the bottom drawer of her desk and stuffed a folder of notes and ideas she had been working on into the bag. Flicking off the office light, she stepped into the darkened hallway, closing the door behind her.

Most everyone was gone for the night. Right now, the school's only occupants would be the security guard, sleepily making his rounds through the dimly lit hallways, and the cleaning crew that faithfully scrubbed the day's accumulation of dirt from the corridors and classroom floors.

She went to the exit doors, stopping long enough to dig her key ring from her bag, and then unlocked the door and stepped into the warm evening air. She carefully locked the door behind her, using the bright streetlight to select her car key from the ring before going into the darkness of the school parking lot.

She glanced down the quiet street. The vehicle that had stopped earlier was no longer there. The park across the street had been vacated, children and sun lovers now nestled securely in their homes for the night.

At the rear of the building, the cleaning crew's van was parked at a service entrance beside the security car, the only vehicles in sight except her own. Her car sat in its usual space, backed up to a high wooden fence at the far end of the lot. It was further to walk, but overhanging trees kept the car cool during hot summer days.

As she neared her vehicle, she pressed the key fob and was welcomed by a pair of beeps and a distinct click as her car doors unlocked.

Behind her, a bright light cast a long shadow ahead of her. The light drew closer and she turned. It was a car. The same car that had been parked across the street from her office a few minutes earlier.

The engine roared as the vehicle gathered speed, heading straight for her. She waved her arms frantically. Didn't he see her?

She froze in the headlights a moment, then her handbag fell from her shoulder as she lunged to one side. She felt a breeze as the car whipped through the spot she'd occupied a moment before. Her handbag tumbled and rolled, destroyed by the tires of the vehicle.

She clambered to her feet, her heart pounding furiously in

her chest. Someone was trying to kill her. Why?

Her body shook all over, her breathing rapid and shallow, and she found it hard to think clearly.

Nina hesitated a moment and then raced toward her car. She stopped short as the driver hit the brakes hard, squealed to a stop on the asphalt, then spun around and stopped. The attacking vehicle faced the side of her car, its headlights flooding the door. As the driver revved the engine, she recoiled in horror.

He was waiting. Waiting for her.

She glanced toward her handbag. Even if she could get to it, her cell phone was probably destroyed, and she could never make it safely into her vehicle before being rammed. The fence behind her car was too high to climb. There was no choice but to run back across the parking lot to the school and hope she could outrun her attacker.

She spun around and sprinted across the lot at full speed. Tires squealed behind her and she glanced over her shoulder. The car moved forward, straight toward her.

She would never make it.

Nina stopped short, turned to face the vehicle, tensed her leg muscles, and held her breath. The car missed her by inches as she dove aside at the last second. She stumbled to her feet as the vehicle braked and circled around for another try.

Her strategy wasn't going to work. She frantically tried to think of a way out of the deadly situation. She raced for the passenger side of her car and tugged at the door handle. The door swung open.

She lunged inside, fell across the front seat, and scrambled to a sitting position. Her eyes bulged and panic overtook her as the other car sped toward her head on. There was a roar, then a crash, as the vehicle swerved and rammed the passenger-side door. It closed with an explosion of shattered glass and twisted metal.

But she was unharmed.

She howled in exasperation coupled with intense fear. Her keys. She had dropped her keys when she'd lost her handbag. She squinted through the windshield and saw them, twenty feet in front of her, glinting in the soft moonlight. And off to her left, the deadly car relentlessly persisted, lined up to T-bone her vehicle on the driver side.

There was no protection, no way of starting the vehicle, and no one to help. She dove headlong through the empty window, gouging her side on a shard of glass as she scrambled to escape the death trap.

She landed hard on her shoulder and hit her head on the asphalt. She lay still a moment, stunned, trying to clear her senses and catch her breath as the attacking vehicle roared somewhere close by.

Her keys. She had to get her keys.

She stumbled to her feet, dazed and hurting, and staggered toward her key ring. It was her only chance. She'd dodged the vehicle once and she could do it again. She would grab her keys, make it to her car, and get as quickly and as far away as possible.

Nina raced to her keys, crouched down, and scrambled to pick them up as tires squealed behind her. She turned to face the killing machine, its headlights nearly blinding her as it roared closer. She waited, poised, and ready.

Now.

Too late. The deadly machine struck her, knocking her off her feet and tossing her to the asphalt. She landed on her back, stunned and unable to move. One leg felt broken, the other weak and useless. She attempted to think clearly, to still the panic overwhelming her senses.

Tires squealed again. An engine raced.

She struggled to sit but fell back on her elbows. As she gazed helplessly toward the oncoming vehicle, she saw her murderer's face for the first time, illuminated by the moonlight.

It was a face she recognized. A face from years ago.

CHAPTER 2

DAY 2 - Tuesday, 6:25 a.m.

ANNIE LINCOLN AWOKE early and her eyes popped open. She took a deep, gasping breath and stared at the ceiling in the dim bedroom. Getting back to sleep was the last thing on her mind, the first thing being the horrendous nightmare she had endured.

She was bound by rusty chains on the fourth floor of a dilapidated mansion, somewhere in a secluded spot, deep in a dark forest. Blood-red tears trickled from the eyes of her abductor as he watched her, his painted lips curled into a sadistic smile. He held up a blood-stained knife and promised to cut off her fingers, one at a time, until she told him the truth.

She had no idea what the truth was or what he wanted to know. She felt no pain as the bloody knife cut through her fingers, and she watched them fall to the floor at his feet, wondering if she would be able to replace them.

It was somewhere around the seventh finger when she awoke, her trembling body covered in chilling sweat. She brought her hands up. Even in the dim room, she saw her fingers were all there, and she breathed again.

She turned her head. Jake was still fast asleep, a contented look on his face, oblivious to what she'd endured. Looking at him made her feel secure, and her shaky chills subsided. She rolled out of bed, her mind foggy, and staggered to the shower. She let the steaming water wash the horrifying memories away.

She wondered if her nightmare had a meaning, or if they were dregs of the worst experiences her mind held. Lately, along with her husband, she'd had more than her fair share of those.

When Jake had been laid off, they'd transformed her successful freelance research business into Lincoln Investigations. It had taken awhile to get the new firm established, but now, the small Canadian city of Richmond Hill they called home supplied more than enough clients to keep them busy. As well as tame chores like background checks and research for regular clientele, they often encountered villains of all varieties.

She stepped from the shower, wrapped herself in a comfortable towel, and blow-dried her shoulder-length hair. She frowned and squinted in the mirror. Perhaps she was mistaken, but for a moment, she thought she saw a gray hair sprouting among the blond. Must've been the light.

By the time she got back to the bedroom, Jake was already stirring, his six-foot-four inch body almost reaching both ends of the bed. She leaned over and helped him wake up with a kiss on his warm lips. He opened his eyes and his warm lips turned into a warm grin.

"Good morning," he said. He rubbed his hand through his short dark hair, then stretched, yawned, groaned once, and asked, "Sleep okay?"

"Slept great," she lied, straightening her back. Actually, it was mostly the truth, except for her early-morning nightmare, now fading away.

She felt Jake's eyes on her while she dressed, and then he tumbled out of bed and yawned as she left the room.

Seeing their eight-year-old son always brought another bright point to her day. She padded into his bedroom and gently jiggled him awake. Matty opened his eyes, rolled over, and lay still. One of these days they would get him an alarm clock so he could get himself out of bed.

"Let's go, Matty. Time to get up."

"I'm up," he said, and she knew he would soon crawl out of bed, get dressed, and appear in the kitchen, ready for breakfast before trudging off to school.

She went downstairs to the kitchen, stood at the sink, and gazed out on the fresh new morning. The early sun shone down from a cloudless sky, promising another beautiful day. She didn't want to waste it by staying inside, but work waited in the office. After breakfast, there were some urgent background checks to do for a client.

Jake came down the stairs, said good morning again, and then went to the basement. His vigorous workout routine would take him a half hour, then after a shower, he would be starving and waiting eagerly for something to eat.

As she started breakfast for herself and her guys, she thought about a phone call she had received the day before. A woman was adamant her husband was having an affair and she didn't know where to turn. Annie had told the woman she'd call back the next day. Jake wasn't too keen on stakeouts, but she wanted to run it by him before she made a decision.

After breakfast was out of the way, Jake helped Annie wash up the dishes while Matty got ready for school. North Richmond Public was only two blocks away, and Matty usually walked there with his best friend from next door. Kyle was a year younger than he, an inch shorter, and the son of Annie's good friend, Chrissy.

Kyle banged on the back door, Matty let him in and the two boys ran upstairs. They would have a while to hang out before they needed to leave for school.

Jake was making a pot of coffee. Annie dried her hands on a towel and left the kitchen. She poked her head back in. "I might have a job for you," she said and left again.

"Be there in a minute," he called.

Annie went into the small office off the living room and booted up the iMac. While she waited, she slid over a file folder and flipped it open.

The woman who suspected her husband of cheating had

sounded heartbroken on the phone, positive she knew who her husband's lover was. If true, that knowledge might make this case a whole lot easier to take care of. Besides, there was nothing urgent for Jake to do at the moment.

The name of the woman was Crystal McKinley, a part-time retail clerk. Her husband was Jeffrey, a criminal defense lawyer.

Jake walked slowly into the office, balancing two cups of coffee filled to the brim. He set one in front of Annie, took a seat in the guest chair, and sipped at his hot drink.

Annie flipped the folder around and slid it toward him. "How would you like to catch a cheating spouse?"

Jake took another sip, set his coffee on the desk, and picked up the folder. He opened it and scanned the single page inside. "Names. Addresses. Everything's here." He looked at Annie. "What does she need us for?"

"She needs proof," Annie said with a shrug. "They always want proof."

Jake nodded slowly. "Okay, I'll get it for her." He closed the folder and tossed it onto the desk. "Should we go see her first?"

"So, we'll take the case?" Annie asked.

"We'll take the case."

Annie picked up the phone and called Mrs. McKinley, drumming her fingers on the desktop while she waited. Three rings later, a woman answered.

"Crystal McKinley?" Annie asked.

"Yes."

"It's Annie Lincoln."

There was silence on the phone, then a whispered voice said, "My husband is still home."

"May we drop by and see you this morning about nine thirty?"

"Yes, that's fine," the hushed voice said, and then the line went dead.

Annie hung up. "Her husband's still home. She can't talk, but nine thirty is good."

Matty poked his head into the office. "We're going to school now."

"Have a great day," she called, and he was gone. Annie heard the front door open and then close a moment later.

She looked at her watch. They still had plenty of time before their appointment with Crystal McKinley. In the meantime, she would get a few small tasks out of the way.

CHAPTER 3

Tuesday, 8:25 a.m.

JASON PUTTWATER was only a lowly substitute teacher, always ready to fill in when the regular teacher didn't show. Whether their absences were because of real illness or feigned, Jason didn't ask or care. He was there. He loved kids and planned to be a full-time teacher someday soon. He had all the qualifications—he was a hard worker who had tons of degrees and the desire to teach.

His ambition, to put it the way he'd been taught in teacher's college, was to ensure today's students become the productive, well-adjusted adults of tomorrow.

At any rate, he was young and determined to shoot for what he deemed to be a worthy goal.

He pulled into the school driveway and waved at the principal, who was climbing down from his Range Rover, parked in a preferred spot by the front door. The principal paid him no mind, brushing an invisible fleck of dust from the front fender of his machine. He buffed it with his sleeve and strode the other way, swinging his black leather Gucci briefcase.

Being a substitute teacher, Jason didn't qualify for any of the half-dozen parking spots by the front door. No, he had to park all the way at the back of the lot beside the office staff and the handful of other substitutes.

He didn't care all that much, anyway. It gave him something to gripe and complain about when there was nothing else to gripe and complain about. Not that he liked to gripe and complain, but sometimes you had to let it all out. No use allowing it to build up inside. Not that it ever did.

Jason liked to arrive early for no good reason. He just did. He usually parked along the back row and was inside the school before anyone else, but today, as he gazed toward the back of the lot, he saw another vehicle in his favorite spot, right underneath an overhanging oak, stealing all the shade.

It also appeared someone had dumped a bag of garbage on the lot not far from the back fence. People had a habit of doing that sometimes. He would drag it over to the utility door on his walk to the school and dump it into the chute. If he didn't do it, nobody else would. He didn't mind.

The only thing was, as he drove closer, it started not to look like a bag of garbage at all, but rather had the shape of a human body. As he bumped along in his ten-year-old Honda, he leaned forward and peered through the windshield. His eyes grew wider and wider, finally bulging almost as large as his gaping mouth when he drew closer to the object.

He touched the brakes hard, his mouth still open, his breathing stopped, and he stared in disbelief.

He shook his head, threw the car in park, and swung from the vehicle. He approached the body slowly, glancing around several times at nothing in particular, and finally stopped five feet from the bloody spectacle.

He breathed now, a lot of breaths, rapid and shallow ones. His throat felt constricted, but he couldn't turn his eyes away from the horrendous sight on the asphalt in front of him.

It was a woman, he was pretty sure of that. At least, it had long dark hair and high heels. Well, one high heel. The other one was missing, the remaining one only halfway on the stockinged foot. The dark hair had streaks and patches of red in it, and Jason knew it wasn't professionally done like a lot of women seemed to be doing these days. Nope. Those streaks were blood, and it wasn't just in her hair, but all over her clothes and the surrounding pavement.

The face was nose-down to the asphalt, the long, bloody hair fanning in all directions. One arm and both legs were twisted in awkward positions, perhaps snapped in more than one place.

Jason hadn't seen such a bloody mess since he was twelve years old and used to blow the crap out of groundhogs and rabbits with his father's old shotgun.

But what caught Jason's bulging eyes was a strange pattern of blood by the woman's right hand. To him, it looked like she'd tried to use a finger to write something in her own blood. He moved around the mangled body, crouched down, and cocked his head.

Yeah, it was writing. It was a scrawl to be sure, but what else could you expect from someone in her condition? The scrawl said, "Adam Thor," but the "r" trailed off like she had taken her last breath before she finished it.

Adam Thor. Strange name—if indeed it was a name. What else could it be? Had to be a name. Maybe it was her killer's name. Jason had heard about people doing that kind of thing before. The dying person's last message.

He stood, moved back a couple of feet, and stared at the horrifying mess. It seemed to him the only way something like this could've happened was by getting run over by a vehicle. Perhaps a couple of times; it was hard to tell. It was overkill, that was for sure.

It was either a case of road rage, or parking lot rage in this case, or somebody had wanted this person dead. Or both. Either way, it was like nothing Jason had ever seen before, and he glanced uneasily around again.

He scratched his head, wondering if the vehicle parked in his spot had something to do with this whole nasty affair. He looked down at the body. It wasn't going anywhere real soon; he might as well take a look at the car.

Even before he reached the vehicle, he could see the mangled passenger-side door. It had more than likely been rammed by the same vehicle that had run over the poor woman over there. He went to the side door and stopped. The window was broken out and glass lay all over the ground and inside the car.

He'd better not get too close or touch anything. The cops wouldn't take too kindly to anyone messing up the crime scene. He knew that much.

He hoped he hadn't trampled on any of the blood around the body. He checked the bottoms of his shoes. Nope. It seemed to be all right.

He strode back to the mess on the ground, stared at the body a moment longer, and then figured it was probably time to call the cops.

CHAPTER 4

Tuesday, 8:43 a.m.

ADAM THORBURN sat on the edge of his bed, dropped his head back, and yawned. Another sleepless night was past. He hated not being able to sleep and wished he could pop a pill and pass out for the night.

But his mother had been firm about that. He was on enough medication as it was, and a sleeping pill, along with his antipsychotic medications, could cause a bad reaction.

He hated the term *antipsychotic*. It made it sound like he was psychotic, but he wasn't. He was schizophrenic—a huge difference. But he hated being schizophrenic too. At only twenty-three years old, he would have to put up with it for a good long time. The doctor said he'd have it for the rest of his life.

Adam yawned again, brushed back his bristling dark hair with one hand, and stood. He was supposed to be at work by nine but would never make it. He was tired of pushing supermarket carts around, anyway. Not that he was lazy. Far from it. He just didn't see any future in it, and frankly, didn't see much of a future for himself at all.

He hated walking to work, too. It only took twenty minutes or so, but it was an annoyance. He'd had a driver's license and an old beat-up Ford when he was younger, but they'd taken his license away years ago. They said it wasn't safe for him to drive.

But his mother insisted he work at whatever job he could land, and he complied—most of the time. She said they needed the money. Her skimpy paycheck barely paid for the basic necessities, and his medication was a drain on the family budget.

Not that it was much of a family. Just him and his mother. His father had been dead for almost a year now. He'd usually gotten along pretty well with his father, but when the old man had been drunk, his father had had some awful arguments with his mother. Seemed like they were at each other's throats a lot of the time.

Adam pulled on his jeans, yesterday's socks, and a faded t-shirt. His shirts barely fit anymore. The paunch he'd developed made sure of that. He wasn't really fat, but he'd put on an extra twenty pounds or so lately, and it was showing in his face as well.

He didn't care all that much about how he looked anymore. Mostly, he hung around all day, worked at the supermarket for a while, and wasted the rest of the time. He had no friends. He hoped to find a girlfriend someday, but that was almost laughable. What girl would want to hang around with a schizo? Maybe another schizo. Adam laughed aloud. What a great combination that would be. They could have little schizo babies. What fun.

The thing that irked him most about other people was they thought he was mentally challenged—retarded, they called him. But he had an above-average IQ, wasn't all that bad looking despite the extra weight, and could usually carry on an intelligent conversation. If he was antisocial, it was because they made him that way. It affected his schoolwork to such a degree, he'd dropped out to get away from the bullies and the so-called normal people who shunned him.

To make things worse, he'd been having more and more blackouts lately. There were periods of time when he had no idea what went on or where he had been. His mother had said it would pass. She insisted that the family was going through a rough time, and it affected him in strange ways. He sure hoped she was right.

Dr. Zalora wasn't much help either. He said pretty much the same thing as his mother—"The death of his father caused him additional problems. It'll get easier in time, and the periods of blackouts will vanish. Take the medication and you'll do fine," was all the doctor had said.

"Adam." It was his mother calling from downstairs.

He opened the bedroom door. "Be down in a minute," he called.

Adam went into the bathroom in the hallway, splashed

20

some water on his face, and wiped it dry, taking a last look at himself in the mirror. He ran a comb through his hair. It didn't do anything; his hair was too short.

When he went downstairs, his mother was waiting for him in the kitchen, sitting forward at the kitchen table, her arms resting on top, her fingers woven together. He stopped short at her unsmiling face.

"Sit down," she said. Her eyes were angry, her voice stern. Something was up.

Adam sat at the other end of the table and leaned forward, his hands on his knees. "What's going on?"

She spoke in an accusing voice. "Where'd you go last night?"

Adam frowned, thinking hard. "I didn't go anywhere. I watched TV while you were gone, then I went to bed."

"Did you have another blackout?" she asked, her tone unchanged.

"I ... I don't think so. I don't always remember when I do."

She sighed and sat back, her eyes drilling into his, her lips in a firm line.

"Is everything all right?" Adam asked.

His mother shook her head. "You smashed up my car," she said. "I shouldn't have left the keys lying around, but I never thought—"

Adam interrupted. "Are you saying I took your car out?"

She sighed again. "I'm afraid you did. I had a few beers last night with Mabel and got home late. I didn't see the damage when I got back, but this morning, there it was." She

How did you get how.

shrugged. "The front is smashed up."

Adam took a sharp breath and held it. He must have had another blackout. Sometimes he did crazy things during the blackouts, and now he'd smashed up his mother's car.

He let out his breath slowly. "I'm sorry, Mom," he said, sinking his head into his hands.

His mother said nothing.

He raised his head and gave her a hopeful look. "Does it still run?"

"I guess it does," she said. "You drove it home again. But it looks like the bumper and one fender is smashed."

He pleaded with his eyes. "I'm really sorry."

She picked at her nail polish, scraping some remnants from a thumb. She brushed the scrapings aside and looked at Adam. "I guess it's not your fault."

He hesitated, then said, "My blackouts are happening more often." He sat back and closed his eyes a moment, taking a deep breath. "I feel like I'm losing my mind sometimes."

"Are you taking your meds?" she asked.

He nodded. "Always."

"All right," she said and stood. "Take a hammer to the fender. See if you can fix it up a bit. It should be okay." She held up a finger. "But don't drive it anywhere."

"I won't."

"Are you not going to work today?"

He shrugged. "I don't feel up to it. I might go in later. They won't fire me. It's too hard to find anyone else to do my lousy job."

She leaned back against the counter and crossed her arms. "Get my car fixed up right away," she said. "I need to go out later. And I can drive you to work if you want to go."

He nodded, avoiding her gaze as she looked at him. Finally, her slippers padded across the floor as she left the kitchen, leaving him alone at the table.

He was worried. He would have to go outside and check out the car. He hoped he hadn't run into another vehicle. That wouldn't be good, but what worried him most was his blackout spells. He didn't hear the voices in his head very often anymore. At least not lately, and he was glad of that. They told him to do some pretty crazy things, and told him some whopping lies, but now it looked like things might've taken a turn for the worse in a different way.

And it frightened him.

CHAPTER 5

Tuesday, 9:04 a.m.

DETECTIVE HANK CORNING steered his Chevy into the Richmond North High School parking lot, waved at an officer controlling access to the area, and was directed toward the rear of the lot. He didn't need to be guided in the right direction. Even from the street, he could see the line-up of police cars parked alongside the forensic van and the ME's vehicle. An ambulance was backed in, its lights still flashing. Other officers kept cars and curious onlookers from the immediate area.

Groups of students, scheduled to be in class, gathered at random places, their curious eyes straining to see the events taking place along the back row of the school parking lot.

It had been a peaceful weekend, giving Hank a chance to catch up on some much-needed sleep and spend quality time with his uncomplaining girlfriend, Amelia. Even yesterday, for a Monday, it was quiet around the precinct, and he had been able to get some paperwork cleaned up. His usually overloaded desk looked organized again.

But at forty years old, and after almost twenty years on the job, he knew peace was short-lived, sparse, and apt to be disrupted at a moment's notice.

It wasn't so much that his peace was disturbed. He was used to that. But what he never got used to was murder, the killing of another human being. As long as ruthless killers preyed on others, his job would never be done.

He pulled up beside an orange cone, one of many cordoning off a large section, and swung from the vehicle. Detective Simon King, Hank's sometime partner, had just arrived in his own car.

King strode over to Hank. "I hear this one's a real mess."

Hank frowned at the other detective, narrowed his deep brown eyes, and disregarded the comment.

King looked like he had just crawled out of bed and slept in his clothes. Hank was pretty sure King wore the same tattered jeans every day with a fresh shirt on occasion. The three days' worth of beard on his face didn't help his look.

The two cops walked over to where a body lay in a tangled heap on the asphalt. Hank stopped a few feet short, a grim look on his face. He sighed deeply and glanced around the lot. Evidence markers were set up in several spots, and a photographer was snapping pictures. CSI would do a thorough job of documenting the scene, their task already well underway.

Lead crime scene investigator Rod Jameson stood nearby, a clipboard in his hand, watching his men as they expertly went about their tasks. The gangling investigator stretched up a couple inches above Hank's six-foot stature, and he nodded his thin head in greeting as the detectives approached.

Hank nodded back and turned his gaze to the body. He'd seen some gruesome murders in the past, slit throats, drownings, hangings, and shootings, but none came close to the horrendous sight in front of him now.

He averted his eyes, took another deep breath, and turned back. The body was mangled almost beyond recognition. There was blood everywhere; most of what the body had once held was puddled and splashed about, much of it soaked into the tattered remnants of clothing that clung to the victim.

A tiny woman, with a frame somewhere between perfect and pudgy, was crouched down doing a preliminary examination of the body, inspecting an arm seemingly broken in several places. It was Medical Examiner Nancy Pietek. She abstained from her normal friendly greeting and glanced up at Hank, a grim look on her usually cheerful round face.

Hank nodded hello, his attention immediately drawn to a series of letters on the pavement apparently written in the victim's own blood. He leaned over and looked closer. "Adam Thor." He took out his cell phone and snapped a close-up of the message.

He crouched down beside Nancy as she brushed aside a

RAYVEN T. HILL

crim

gaze

"

victi

cau

ag

ex

w

]

arm toward the group of cruisers parked fif

name's Jason Puttwater."

Hank glanced to where Jameson i

take a look at the vehicle first." H

King following.

Hank took note of the b

avoided the glass on th

inside. No keys in

examined the m

rammed by an

Nina White

clinging

Ki

we

Hank's benefit, motioning toward an ev... feet away. "Tire track there, Hank. Made from blood."

Hank went over to the cone and examined the distinct crimson track. He turned back. "You have an ID, Rod?"

Jameson handed Hank an envelope. "Here's her driver's license. Name's Nina White. Apparently, she's the school counselor here." He pointed toward the vehicle parked along the back fence. "That vehicle's registered in her name. Found the ownership papers inside."

Hank glanced briefly toward the vehicle, then asked, "Any witnesses?"

Jameson consulted his clipboard. "No witnesses have come forward, but the guy who found the body this morning is waiting with one of the officers." He motioned with a long

y feet away. "His

ndicated, then said, "I'll

e strode toward the fence,

oken passenger-side window. He

e ground and leaned over to look

the ignition. He stepped back and

ngled door. It appeared to have been

other vehicle, likely the one that had killed

He snapped a picture of some flecks of paint

o the door. Black flecks on a white car.

ng leaned in and looked at the door. "I guess that means

need to find a black car with white paint on it."

"Looks like it," Hank said. "And one that matches the tire track and has a dent or two in the front."

"And blood all over it."

"Let's talk to Puttwater," Hank said, striding toward the cruisers.

They found Jason Puttwater leaned against one of the police cars chatting with an officer. Hank introduced himself and King.

"It's a dreadful shame," Puttwater said, straightening his back. "The officer told me who it was." He shook his head and put his hands in his pockets. "Everybody liked Nina. Least, as far as I know."

"Obviously someone didn't," King said.

Puttwater twisted his head and gave King an odd look then turned back to Hank. "Any idea who did this?"

Hank shook his head. "Not yet." He pulled out a pad and

pen from his inner jacket pocket, licked his thumb, and leafed to a blank page. "Tell me how you came to find the body."

"I'm a substitute teacher here at Richmond North High School. I came to work early and found her here."

"Did you touch anything?"

Puttwater shook his head. "Didn't touch a thing. Just looked. Then I called you guys."

"Did you know Nina White?"

"Not really," Puttwater said, shrugging one shoulder. "Talked to her a few times. Said hello, but never knew anything about her."

"Any other vehicles in the area when you got here?" King asked.

"Nope. Just the principal at the front of the school. I was the first to park in the back lot. Except for Nina's car, of course."

Hank got Puttwater's contact information and handed him a business card. "An officer will take your complete statement. Contact me if you can think of anything else."

Puttwater nodded and leaned back against the cruiser.

Hank spoke to King as they walked to their vehicles. "We have to find the maniac who did this, King. See what you can find out. In the meantime, I'd better see if Nina White has any next of kin and pay them a visit."

"I'll get on it, Hank."

Hank watched King return to his vehicle and drive away before going to his Chevy. He figured the fastest way to find out more about Nina White was to visit the school office, which would undoubtedly have the information he needed to perform the uncomfortable task he now faced.

CHAPTER 6

Tuesday, 9:25 a.m.

JAKE EASED THE Firebird past the massive stone-and-wrought-iron gates and glanced up at the sprawling mansion where the McKinleys lived. It was set in the middle of five acres of prime real estate, exquisite landscaping extending in all directions. On the second floor, a huge balcony ran the entire width of the building, overlooking the front of the property.

He exchanged a glance with Annie. He wasn't sure what she thought, but he knew this was a client who could pay. The value of the towering, French chateau-style home had to be in the millions. The four-car garage alone was bigger than their whole house.

He pulled up near the ten-foot-wide brick walkway and stopped the car. They got out and went up the walk, climbing onto a massive outdoor porch supported by a half dozen lofty pillars. Jake clanked the knocker on one of two solid oak doors and stood back.

The door swung open a moment later and a woman appeared in the doorway. Without the extra thirty pounds of weight, she would've been quite beautiful. And even with it, she would have no problem turning a few heads. Her long, wavy black hair alone was worth an admiring glance, as it framed a classic face, made up to perfection.

Jake and Annie introduced themselves and the woman motioned for them to enter. As they stepped inside the foyer, Jake gazed at the hardwood floor lining the main hallway, leading to a massive kitchen at the far end. To his right, a lavish double stairway soared upwards, probably to countless bedrooms.

Crystal McKinley's long, perfectly fitted dress swished as she turned and led them through a wide arched doorway into a living room, extending from the front of the house to rear double doors facing the back of the property. She approached a group of overstuffed chairs, arranged in a circular pattern at the back of the room, and motioned for them to sit.

They sank into plush chairs and Jake glanced through the large rear windows. His eyes roved down a tiered, grassed area, past an Olympic-sized swimming pool, through a garden, to a tennis court beyond.

He turned back and faced Mrs. McKinley. She looked to be in her midforties and sat stiff-backed, her hands clasped together in her lap, her lips unsmiling.

The woman didn't waste any time and got to the heart of her problem after the exchange of a few obligatory pleasantries.

"As I told you on the phone, I know my husband's cheating on me," she said, a dejected look crossing her face.

Jake took another glance around the opulent room. "Your husband's a lawyer, Mrs. McKinley?"

"Yes. He's a successful criminal defense lawyer. Mostly wealthy clients. He's the managing partner at McKinley & Baker."

A light dawned in Jake's head. "I recognize the name now," he said. He was well aware of the man. McKinley had taken the leadership role as a defense attorney on many high-profile cases and the man was almost unbeatable, though many of his clients were known to be on the shady side of the law.

"You mentioned you knew the ... other woman?" Annie asked, removing a notepad and pen from her handbag. She made a note on an empty page.

A darkness appeared in Mrs. McKinley's eyes. "Yes, I do. Her name's Willow Taft and she's a gold digger."

Annie jotted the name in her notepad. "Do you have her address?"

Mrs. McKinley reached a hand toward Annie, pointing toward the notepad. "I can give you her address as well as the address and phone number of my husband's firm."

Annie handed the woman her pad and waited until Mrs. McKinley finished writing and handed it back.

Jake glanced over at the woman's elegant cursive handwriting. She was obviously well educated. The woman had also written down a description of her husband's favorite car, a red Mercedes Roadster—a convertible.

Annie spoke. "Mrs. McKinley, how can you be sure your husband is having an affair?"

The woman sighed. "I went to his office a few days ago when he wasn't there. I suspected it already, but I wasn't sure, so I went through his desk drawers and found a box of condoms. Strange, yes, but not enough." She sighed again, this time deep and long. "So I dug a little further and found photos of that woman. Provocative photos, if you know what I mean."

"Do you know the woman?" Jake asked.

She nodded. "Yes, he had an affair with her a number of years ago and I thought it was long past. But it seems to have been renewed."

"Are you sure they weren't old photos?" Jake asked. "And he kept them for some reason?"

Mrs. McKinley shook her head. "I know he's having an affair. Whenever I give him a hug, I smell strange perfume on him. And his suit jackets have that same smell almost every day." She dropped her eyes. "And ... we rarely make love anymore."

Jake looked at Annie and raised his brows. The woman seemed to have lots of evidence and now she wanted some undeniable proof.

The distraught woman raised her eyes. "I ... I don't want a divorce. I love my husband and I know he loves me. I only want to put an end to this and get our marriage back on track."

Annie spoke. "And you think confronting him with the proof will change him?"

"I hope it will. My husband is a good man, but I'm desperate."

Jake wondered if the woman wanted to avoid a divorce to keep from disrupting her extravagant lifestyle, but a look into Mrs. McKinley's saddened eyes made him change his mind. She seemed to be sincere, trying to soothe her broken heart.

Annie closed the notepad and tucked it into her handbag. "We'll see what we can come up with as soon as possible."

Mrs. McKinley reached to a stand beside her chair and retrieved an envelope. She handed it to Annie. "I hope you don't mind cash? I can't write you a check for obvious reasons. I need to keep this a secret ... for now."

Annie took the envelope, glanced inside, and thumbed quickly through the bills. "Unless this takes longer than we expect, this should be plenty." She closed the envelope and dropped it into her handbag. "Do you want a receipt?"

Mrs. McKinley shook her head and smiled weakly. "You have a good reputation and I don't want a paper trail. I don't think a receipt will be necessary."

"We'll let you know how things go as we proceed," Jake said and looked at Annie. "Anything else we need to know?"

"I believe we have enough information," Annie said. She stood and faced Mrs. McKinley. "I'll contact you if there's anything else we need."

Jake and Mrs. McKinley stood and the woman led them to

the foyer. She opened the door and thanked them, hope in her eyes.

They stepped out onto the porch and the solid door closed behind them.

Inside the car, Annie turned to Jake and patted her handbag. "There's ten thousand dollars in this envelope."

Jake's mouth dropped open. "This woman means business. She must be desperate."

"Wouldn't you be?" Annie asked.

Jake grinned and started the Firebird. "You don't have to worry about that. We're never going to be in this situation."

Annie looked at her watch. "What do you say about getting on this immediately? It's still early and we've got all day."

Jake laughed. "I'm game, but let's not do it too quickly. We've got ten thousand dollars' worth of time to use up." He glanced over at Annie's frown and lost his grin. "Just kidding. We'll give her a refund if necessary."

CHAPTER 7

Tuesday, 10:20 a.m.

HANK SAT IN the office of Richmond North High School, leaning forward in his chair, his hands cupped in front of him. He gazed around the busy room. The administrative staff went about their chores almost as though nothing had happened in the parking lot behind the school.

Occasionally, someone would give him a brief glance, then look away. Two or three would gather, put their heads together, then carry on with their business. Though no one had been informed who the unfortunate victim was, they knew why he was there. He wished he were somewhere else, but someone had to talk to Teddy White, and the unpleasant task always fell in his lap.

He was informed by the principal that Nina White's husband was not at home but had answered his cell and would be in shortly, not to take care of his students, but to talk with the detective, who waited patiently, fidgeting with his hands.

Hank looked over as a man wearing a dark suit and a cinnamon-red tie walked past the counter and glanced around. The principal spied the man and waddled hurriedly across the floor, approaching him. The principal leaned in, spoke some quiet words, and pointed toward Hank, and the man looked Hank's way.

Hank stood as the men approached.

"You may use my office," the principal said.

Hank nodded at the principal and turned toward the unsmiling man. "Teddy White?"

The man leaned in slightly and spoke in a low, stiff voice. "Yes."

"This way," the principal said, motioning toward an office. Hank picked up his briefcase and they followed him, stepping inside the room. The principal left them alone and closed the door quietly.

Hank motioned toward one of two guest chairs on the near side of the desk. Teddy White sat down, crossed his legs, straightened his back, and looked at the detective.

Hank turned the other chair around, sat his briefcase on the floor beside the chair, and sat facing Teddy. The man was in his late forties, his thin face lined with worry. Perspiration gathered on his semi-bald head, his high brow wrinkled with growing fear. He remained silent, his eyes searching Hank's face.

The cop leaned forward, struggling to find the right words, but they never seemed to come. He cleared his throat, leaned in, and spoke softly. "Mr. White, my name's Detective Corning. I'm afraid I have to inform you ..." Hank took a short breath. "It's about your wife. She's been killed."

Teddy White sat unmoving, his worried face unchanged, his eyes glaring into Hank's, trying to process what he just heard. Sometimes it could take awhile to sink in; it never went the same way twice.

Hank waited and watched.

The voice came at last, low, reserved, unemotional. "What happened?"

Hank sat back. "She was hit by a car. Run over." He cocked a thumb over his shoulder. "It happened last night in the parking lot."

Teddy's voice finally cracked. "Run over?"

Hank nodded.

Teddy leaned forward, pain now showing in his eyes. "On purpose?"

"It looks that way," Hank said. "I'm very sorry."

Teddy nodded slightly in recognition of Hank's words. "I was afraid something happened when she didn't come home last night. She's dedicated to her students and often works late, occasionally until two or three in the morning."

"When did you talk to her last?" Hank asked.

Teddy thought a moment, running his fingers through the thin, graying hair above one ear. "Perhaps eight o'clock last night. She called to tell me she would be working late and wasn't sure what time she would be home."

"When did you suspect … something was wrong?"

Teddy sighed deeply and sat back. "I went to bed without her at eleven o'clock. When I woke up at two in the morning, she still wasn't home. I wasn't worried at the time, but I didn't sleep well after that. About five o'clock I gave her a call." He dropped his head. "She didn't answer. I've been on the phone ever since trying to track her down. When the principal called me awhile ago I feared the worst."

Hank remained quiet, unsure what to say.

Teddy looked up. "Where's my wife now?"

"They've taken her to the city morgue." Hank hated to say that. It always sounded so cold. He added, "The medical examiner will inspect her, but the cause of death is clear." Teddy looked distraught, so Hank added, "Your wife's body is in good hands, Mr. White. She'll be treated respectfully."

The man's lower lip trembled, his voice now shaking. "Do you know who did this?"

Hank tightened his lips and shook his head. "Not yet. We'll do all we can. We have some leads and expect to find the person shortly."

A tear escaped and rolled down the man's face. He brushed it away and cleared his throat, his eyes roving unseeing around the office. Finally, he looked back at the detective and narrowed his eyes. "How could anyone do this?"

"That's what we need to find out," Hank said. "Do you have any idea at all who could be responsible?"

Teddy thought a moment, his head shaking slowly back and forth. "I can't even begin to think who it might be. She had no enemies." His voice broke again. "All she ever wanted to do was help people. Especially the students." Another tear fell and was quickly brushed away.

Hank put a hand on Teddy's shoulder. "I'm sorry." He held his hand there awhile and then sat back and sighed.

"Are you sure it was intentional?" Teddy asked, his voice trembling.

Hank's face was grim. "I believe so." He paused. "It looks like she was run over perhaps two or three times."

Teddy's eyes widened and he took a sharp breath, a growing anger in his eyes. Then his brow wrinkled and he asked slowly, "Two or three times?"

"I'm afraid so."

Teddy closed his eyes and dropped his head back. When he opened them again, he looked intently at Hank. "What can I do to help? I'll do anything. Anything at all."

"I'm afraid there's nothing you can do," Hank said. "Unless you can come up with a motive—a reason someone might want to kill your wife—there's little else you can do." He paused. "We'll take care of it, Mr. White."

"How many detectives are on this?"

"There's just the two of us," Hank said. "Myself and Detective King. He's looking into leads now."

Teddy frowned. "Only two? Is there no one else who can help you?"

"I'm afraid not," Hank said. He knew the victim's family was always anxious to find the perpetrator as soon as possible. He understood that, and it was the reason he didn't rest until he found the killer, especially in a case so horrific.

Teddy sat quietly in emotional pain as Hank explained more about how Nina White's heinous murder had taken place. "Her car was taken to the evidence pound for forensic examination as well."

"She loved that car," Teddy said, his eyes far away.

"It'll be returned to you," Hank said.

Teddy looked at Hank and nodded.

Hank opened his briefcase and took out a card, handing it to the man. "You can always reach me here. If you think of anything that might help, or need an update on the case, feel free to call."

Teddy took the card, glanced at it briefly, and tucked it into the inner pocket of his jacket. "Please find out who did this, Detective."

Hank nodded, picked up his briefcase, and stood. "We'll get him," he said, making a promise he shouldn't. "It's my only priority."

The detective followed Teddy from the room, nodded at the principal, and left the building. He had a feeling they could solve this case quickly. There seemed to be plenty of evidence, and he looked forward to seeing what Detective King had come up with.

CHAPTER 8

Tuesday, 10:46 a.m.

ON THE WAY HOME from the McKinley house, Jake and Annie discussed approaches they could take to discover whether or not Jeffrey McKinley was cheating on his wife. They decided to split up. Jake would stake out McKinley, and Annie would see what she could find out about his supposed lover, Willow Taft.

When they arrived home, they went into the house to pick up the necessary equipment—a pair of binoculars each, along with a couple of Nikon digital cameras with zoom lenses. Jake dropped their only compact video camera into his shoulder bag with two bottles of water.

Their destination was downtown, and Annie followed Jake

in her car, then cut off, heading toward Willow Taft's house in a nearby residential area.

Someone as high-profile and in as much demand as Jeffrey McKinley wouldn't be easy to get to. Jake called McKinley & Baker and was informed Mr. McKinley was in a meeting and would be unavailable the rest of the day. His helpful secretary offered to set up an appointment sometime next week. Jake declined politely. He didn't need to visit the man anyway; he just wanted to determine his whereabouts.

He continued toward the heart of the city. Parking was limited, and he circled the block twice before finding a spot on the side street across from his destination. He got out of his vehicle, slung the bag onto his shoulder, and crossed the street.

McKinley & Baker was on the seventh floor of a high-rise office building, one of only a few that made up the small skyline. It wasn't a large city, but it was growing steadily, the downtown core ever modernizing itself.

He strolled to the back of the building and approached the entrance to the underground parking lot. Vehicle access was granted to cardholders only, but he slipped by the gate into the brightly lit modern parking facility.

It didn't take him long to find McKinley's red Mercedes convertible, parked in a reserved spot on the main parking level near the exit doors leading to the lobby. He tried the lobby door. It was locked. He would either need a key or a keycard to gain access, but at least he knew McKinley was in the building.

He left the underground area by the way he'd come,

walked out to Main Street, and approached the front of the towering structure. He strode through the revolving door and into the lobby of the luxurious building, lit by an iconic chandelier and pendant lamps that adorned the high ceiling.

A constant flow of drones crisscrossed each other's paths across the Italian marble floor, scurrying to get their urgent business done. A few workers from the retail outlets that lined the sides of the massive lobby were on break, enjoying a snack or a cup of coffee on the hard stone benches by the tranquil fountain.

Jake sat on one of the deluxe armchairs at one side of the foyer. He had a perfect view of the doors leading to the underground parking. He pulled out his phone and did a quick search, bringing up numerous stories about the successful lawyer. Jake was able to find a clear picture of the man, clad in an Armani suit, shaking hands with the mayor.

More than handsome, McKinley had spectacular looks, warm, blue eyes, and a smile that could distract anyone. He often used that charm on the jury in court, and now it seemed he was using it on Willow Taft.

Jake gave Annie a call. "I'm in the lobby of his building now," he told her, watching a couple of suits stroll by as they carried on an intense discussion. "His car's here, so I'll wait awhile and watch for him to leave."

"I'm sitting across the street from Willow Taft's house," Annie said. "She was out shopping. She just got home and carried a whole load of shopping bags inside. And I don't mean groceries. The bags looked like they were from high-end fashion stores."

"Probably out spending McKinley's money," Jake said. "With the kind of money he makes, he can easily afford to keep two women."

"Give me a call if he leaves. And if she goes out again, I'll follow her. Mrs. McKinley suspects they're having a daily rendezvous, so I don't want her to slip away."

Jake hung up, yawned, and sank back into the chair. He was prepared for a long wait.

Two hours later, Jake almost wished they hadn't taken this case. Another phone call to Annie confirmed she hadn't budged from her spot either, and Willow Taft was still at home.

Then a few minutes later, the elevator doors dinged open and McKinley stepped out carrying a briefcase, heading for the parking area. Jake sat forward. Finally he would have some action. He was bored and stiff from sitting so long.

He sprang from his seat, hurried out the front door, and got to his car as McKinley turned from the lot, heading for Main. Jake jumped in and started the Firebird, spun it around, and followed.

He called Annie. "He's on his way somewhere," he told her when she answered. "I'm following him, and if he's headed your way, you should see him in about ten minutes."

McKinley was headed north, Jake not far behind, keeping a car between him and the object of his attention. The guy was headed in the right direction at least.

McKinley breezed through an orange light. Jake pulled up quickly as the car in front of him stopped. He peered through the windshield. McKinley would soon be out of sight.

When the light turned green, Jake touched the gas and spun around the car in front of him, breaking a couple of traffic laws in the process. But McKinley was nowhere to be seen. Either he was far ahead or he had turned off somewhere.

He called Annie. "I lost him, but we're nearby. I know a shortcut, so I should be there in a couple of minutes. If he's heading your way, it should be a close call."

The engine of the Firebird roared as Jake took a left turn and touched the gas. Several turns later, he was on the quiet street where Willow Taft lived. He saw Annie's car. He zipped past her, pulled down the next street, and parked around the corner, safely out of sight of Willow's house. He grabbed his shoulder bag, jumped out, and raced back around the corner.

McKinley's Mercedes eased down the street from the other direction. Jake slowed to a casual walk until he reached Annie's car. He opened the passenger-side door and jumped in as McKinley pulled into Willow's driveway across the street.

Annie gave Jake a quick glance, a hi, and a smile, then turned her attention back to the camera. She continued to snap pictures as Jake dug the video camera from the shoulder bag and switched it on. He trained it on the Mercedes and zoomed in.

McKinley stepped out, a cell phone in his hand. He tucked it into his pocket, then took a quick look up and down the street as he removed his jacket. He tossed it into the backseat of the car, straightened his tie, brushed back his slick hair, and strode to the front door without another glance. Jake had a perfect view from where they sat, and the video camera continued to catch the scene.

McKinley rang the bell and stepped back, taking a vague glance around as he waited.

And then the door opened and Jake zoomed in.

Willow Taft stood in the doorway, dressed in a negligee, a smile on her attractive face. She reached out her arms and McKinley stepped into the foyer, then into her embrace, and she welcomed him with a passionate kiss. Willow reached over his shoulder and closed the door behind him.

"We got him," Annie said.

"We sure did," Jake said. "But it's not hard and fast proof of infidelity and might not hold up in court. Any good lawyer, especially McKinley, would argue it's only circumstantial. He could say he's visiting a client."

"We're not in court," Annie said. "I'm sure it'll be enough for Crystal McKinley."

CHAPTER 9

Tuesday, 12:54 p.m.

HANK PARKED his Chevy behind the precinct, grabbed his briefcase from the passenger seat, and stepped out. King's car was in its usual spot, and Hank hoped the detective had done a little work on the case. King had come into the school building as Hank was leaving, and Hank had assigned him a few research tasks to take care of.

He strode through the double doors and glanced around the precinct floor. King was not in sight. He was probably in the break room, one of his usual haunts. Hank went straight to his desk, put his briefcase beside his chair, then sat and pulled himself up to the desk.

It would take forensics a while to get a complete report on

the Nina White case, but he was pleased to see the preliminary report waiting for him. The ME's report would be a while yet. Hank didn't envy Nancy's job of sorting this one out. He assumed she had no world-shaking evidence—otherwise she would've notified him immediately.

He opened the folder and browsed through the papers. Nina White's car, including the trunk, had been searched and its contents itemized. Nothing special there. The contents of her purse were listed, including a broken cell phone. Forensics was still trying to see what was on the phone.

He browsed a set of photographs. There were several of the body, close-ups of the tire track, and shots of the black paint on Nina's vehicle. He paused at the photo of Nina's writing in her own blood on the asphalt. Adam Thor. That's where he would start.

He spun his chair around and wheeled over to a nearby desk. Detective Callaway, the technical whiz in residence, looked up as Hank dropped the photo onto his desk.

"What do we have here, Hank?" Callaway asked, removing his hands from the keyboard and picking up the picture.

"I need whatever you can find on this name," Hank said, pointing to Nina's message. "It's probably not a complete name. By the way the *r* trails off, it looks like she wasn't able to finish."

"I'll get on it right away," Callaway said. "I have to clean up something here. Give me five minutes."

Hank spun back to his desk. If the killer's car was the one that smashed up the door of Nina's vehicle, then they were looking for a black car with a dent on it, matching the tire track from the photo, and perhaps with some remnants of blood still on the tire. Possibly registered to someone named Adam with a last name beginning with "Thor." There might also be a powdering of glass on the hood of the vehicle from the broken window in Nina White's car.

Hank looked up as an intern approached his desk. "This is from Dr. Pietek," the intern said, holding out an evidence bag.

Hank took the bag and held it up. He frowned. It looked like a bud from a rose—a red rose. He read the description and Nancy's remarks on the outside of the bag. During her examination of the body of Nina White, the rose had been found in the mouth of the victim.

He laid the bag on his desk, took out his cell phone, and snapped a close-up shot of the flower. He sat back and crossed his arms. What was the significance of the rose? Surely it meant something. The killer had tried to send a message of some kind, that much seemed obvious.

Had the killer run over his victim, then gotten out of the car and placed the rose in her mouth? If so, the victim was probably still alive at the time and had lived long enough after to scratch the message in her own blood. Otherwise, the killer would've seen the message and erased it.

As far as he knew, CSI hadn't found any footprints at the scene or they would've notified him.

Detective King came over to Hank's desk, a coffee in one hand, a muffin in the other. He dropped into a chair and leaned back, sipping at his drink.

Hank looked up. "Got anything?"

King took another sip of his coffee and sat it on the edge of Hank's desk. "I talked to all the teachers and everyone at the school who knew Nina White. They were all shocked, of course, but nobody could give me any idea who might want her dead."

"That's pretty much what her husband said. She didn't have an enemy in the world."

Hank waited until King devoured the last bite of his muffin and washed it down with a long slug of coffee. King wiped his hands on his jeans and took a breath.

"I also went through the student database with the school secretary," he said. "There's no one enrolled there at the moment with the name of Adam, and no Adam Thor."

"Anything else?"

"Yup. I went through Nina's filing cabinet as well as her computer. She has information on all the students she counsels. Still came up dry. Nothing remotely resembling Adam Thor."

Hank glanced over at Callaway. The cop was leaned into his monitor. "Callaway's looking into the name," Hank said. "He'll find something." He handed King the evidence bag containing the rose. "What do you make of this?"

King took the bag and squinted at the contents. "It's a rose," he said.

"Obviously," Hank said. "But it was found in the mouth of the victim. Any idea what it might mean?"

King held up the bag and frowned at the flower. He shook his head slowly, then his eyes brightened. "A red rose represents love and romance. Maybe the killer was in love with the victim, she turned him down, and he wasn't too happy about it." He shrugged. "He might be saying, 'If I can't have you, nobody can.'"

Hank thought about that. "It's a good theory. And if it's true, then this Adam Thor is someone she knew well. Perhaps he'd been stalking her. She obviously knew him well enough to know his name."

Callaway came over to Hank's desk. He carried a printout and he slid it in front of Hank. "I went through all the vehicle registrations for variations on the name Adam Thor but found nothing within a fifty-mile radius."

Hank looked at the printout. "Then what's all this?"

"I kept looking," Callaway said. "I searched within fifty miles for any vehicles registered in a last name beginning with 'Thor.' I narrowed the search down to only black vehicles and came up with two possibilities."

Hank ran his finger down the page. "Virginia Thorburn and James Thorbury."

Callaway continued, "James Thorbury lives out of town and he's a judge. Not a likely suspect, but not impossible."

"And Virginia Thorburn?" Hank asked.

"Virginia Thorburn lives north of town. Number 112 Mill Street. Owns a black 2005 Honda Accord." Callaway paused. "And here's the kicker. She has a twenty-three-year-old son. Are you ready? His name's Adam Thorburn."

Hank sat back and folded his arms, looking at King. "Could be him. Driving his mother's car." Hank looked at Callaway. "Does he still live with his mother?"

"From what I could find out, yes, he does." Callaway

pointed to the paper in Hank's hand. "And he was a student at Richmond North High School. Dropped out seven years ago without graduating."

Hank sat forward and smiled grimly. "That's gotta be him. Explains why King couldn't find anything in the school records or Nina's White's files." He looked up. "Thanks, Callaway. Good job."

"Need anything else, just let me know, guys. You know where to find me," Callaway said as he turned away.

"Looks like we have enough for a search warrant, King," Hank said. "Let's get everything together and talk to a judge. And we'll bring Thorburn in for some serious questioning."

CHAPTER 10

Tuesday, 1:27 p.m.

WITH THE EVIDENCE Hank had accumulated, he was able to get an immediate warrant allowing a search of the house and property where Adam Thorburn lived, including the vehicle Hank suspected had been used as the murder weapon.

Two police cruisers, along with the two detectives following in Hank's car, made their way silently down the street and pulled in front of a beat-up house in a run-down neighborhood. A search team was close behind, ready at Hank's signal to do a meticulous search of the property.

The squat bungalow at 112 Mill Street was one of many in this time-worn community on the edge of town, the dwellings erected decades ago, long forgotten by progress that had torn down and rebuilt other areas of the growing city. Home to the uneducated and the unlucky, ownership in this neighborhood was cheap, the rent even cheaper, and the occupants stubbornly clung to their habitations.

Or perhaps it was because no one wanted to buy cheap, tear down the old, and build bigger, in this undesirable community with nothing but riffraff for neighbors. The nearby steel mill, long criticized for pumping out toxic fumes, was an additional deterrent to much-needed renewal.

As officers sprang from their vehicles and surrounded the house, Hank and King got out and approached a black 2005 Honda Accord parked in the driveway. Hank went immediately to the front of the vehicle.

"Looks like the one," he said, pointing to a scratched bumper and a smashed fender. He crouched down and examined the bumper. Amid the scratches, flecks of white paint were visible. He examined the fender and saw more flecks of white paint.

Once CSI matched up the tire treads with the track from the murder scene and examined the tires for traces of Nina White's blood, they'd have their proof and their man.

Officers were now at the front and back of the house. Hank strode to the side door, King following. They drew their weapons and Hank banged on the door.

"RHPD. Open the door," Hank called.

He heard a rustling and the door moved inward, scraping along the floor as it opened. A woman in her late thirties appeared in the doorway. Her mouth dropped open and she raised her hands halfway, then took a step back, an astonished look on her face.

Hank held up the warrant in his free hand. "I have a warrant to search these premises."

The woman's large eyes became larger and she lowered her hands, clasping them above the waist of her tight, short skirt, her low-cut blouse revealing an immodest amount of cleavage. Cheap costume jewelry adorned her neck and one wrist. Gaudy earrings swung under her long brown hair, all in sharp contrast to her faded and worn slippers.

Hank moved inside and the woman stepped back, allowing him to enter the kitchen.

"Does Adam Thorburn live here?" Hank asked, glancing around the room.

She nodded uncertainly. "Yes ... yes, but he's not here right now."

"Are you Mrs. Thorburn?" King asked.

"Yes. I'm Virginia Thorburn. Why're you looking for Adam?"

Hank didn't answer. He waved an officer inside to stay with Mrs. Thorburn as the detectives went through the house, clearing each room, searching for the suspect.

Adam Thorburn was not there.

Hank approached Mrs. Thorburn. "Where is he, ma'am?"

"I ... I don't know. What's this all about?"

Hank paused and looked at the distraught woman. "Your son is suspected of murder."

She gasped and a hand went to her painted mouth. "It's not possible," she said. "Adam would never hurt anyone."

"Does your son work?"

"Yes ... sometimes, but I don't think he went in today."

"And you don't know where he is?"

She shook her head.

A search team had moved into the house. They would look for weapons as well as anything connecting Adam Thorburn to the crime.

Mrs. Thorburn dropped into a chair at the table, lines of worry now on her brow, her hands in her lap as she watched the proceedings. She looked at Hank as he sat at the other end of the table and removed a pad and pen from his pocket.

"Where does Adam work?" Hank asked.

"Mortino's."

"What does he do there?"

"He brings in the grocery carts people leave outside."

"Do you work, Mrs. Thorburn?"

She nodded. "I'm a waitress. I work evenings, four days a week at a bar two blocks away."

"Did you work last night?"

"Just Thursday through Sunday." She shrugged. "The place isn't busy enough the rest of the time."

Hank made a notation in his pad then pulled out his phone. He found the number for Mortino's, called the store, and was notified Adam Thorburn was not at work today. He was assured by the manager Hank would receive an immediate call if Adam was heard from or came into work.

Hank hung up and looked at Mrs. Thorburn. She was watching the search team as they browsed through cupboards and rifled through drawers.

"Mrs. Thorburn," Hank asked, "did Adam go out last night with the car?"

She turned back, leaned in, and clasped her hands in front of her on the table. She dropped her eyes a moment, then raised them toward Hank, nodding her head briefly. "I was next door and came home late. But this morning, I saw Adam had taken the car out while I was away."

"You noticed it was smashed up on the front?" Hank asked.

She nodded. "Yes. That's how I knew Adam took it."

"Does he drive it often?"

She shook her head. "No. He doesn't have a license anymore. They ... took it away from him."

Hank leaned in. "Who took it away?"

She took a deep breath. "His doctor notified MOT that Adam has schizophrenia and it's not safe for him to drive."

Hank sat back and narrowed his eyes. "Why is it not safe?"

"He has delusions and hallucinations on occasion. And lately, periods when he blacks out entirely and doesn't remember anything." She frowned deeply. "Did Adam have an accident?"

"We believe he ran over someone. A woman."

She tilted her head slightly. "But you said murder?"

Hank looked at the woman, distraught, worried, and fearful for her son. "It looks like he might've done it on purpose."

She shook her head adamantly and spoke in a firm voice. "Never."

"Perhaps there's another explanation," Hank said. "But it's important we find him."

She nodded and dropped her eyes toward her fidgeting hands.

Hank stood and went outside where CSI was examining the Honda. He approached an investigator who crouched by a front tire, scraping at a tread with a special tool. The investigator looked at Hank and said, "There appear to be traces of blood between the treads."

Once the blood was examined, Hank was certain it would prove to be that of Nina White. "Do the treads match up with the track at the scene?" he asked.

"A visual examination tells me they're similar, but I can't tell for certain yet, Hank. Once we get the vehicle back and do a computer analysis of the tire, I'm betting we'll find it's the right car."

The vehicle would shortly be transported back to the lab for further examination, carried on a flatbed truck to avoid disturbing evidence. But Hank felt certain they had the right vehicle and the right man, and he hoped the BOLO he'd issued on Adam Thorburn would soon bring him in.

He turned and walked around to the back of the dwelling and stopped short. He wasn't a botanical expert by any means, but the red rosebuds on the plants along the rear wall of the house looked like the one found in Nina White's mouth.

He plucked off a bud and tucked it into an evidence bag. The lab would know whether or not the two buds were the same species.

But even without that comparison, Hank knew they had more than enough evidence.

Now all he needed to do was find Adam Thorburn.

CHAPTER 11

Tuesday, 1:55 p.m.

ANNIE HAD CALLED Crystal McKinley on her cell phone as soon as they arrived home. The woman was out, but she arranged to meet Annie at a small cafe off Main Street at two o'clock.

Annie printed out several of the most incriminating photos and tucked them inside a manila envelope along with the flash drive containing the video. She grabbed her handbag and poked her head into the kitchen, where Jake sat at the table, browsing the newspaper.

"I'll be back in twenty minutes," she said, holding up the envelope. "I'm going to give this to Mrs. McKinley."

"What about a refund?" Jake asked. "It didn't take us all that long."

"We'll see," Annie said. "I'll offer most of it back." She turned her head as the office phone rang, then looked at her watch. She was running close on time. Maybe she should let the call go to voicemail. She changed her mind and dashed into the office, answering the phone.

"Lincoln Investigations. This is Annie Lincoln."

"Ms. Lincoln. Hello. My name's Teddy ... Teddy White."

Annie sat and pulled her chair in to the desk. "Yes, Mr. White. How can I help you?"

"My wife was ... killed yesterday. Murdered. I've talked to the detective several times. He said they have a suspect."

"You would be better to let the police handle it, Mr. White. If they have enough evidence, they'll make an arrest."

Teddy White sighed and his voice shook as he talked. "The murderer has disappeared, and I don't think they're doing enough to find him. At first the detective wouldn't tell me who it was, but I persisted, and he gave me the man's name."

Annie hesitated. She knew most victims are content to wait until the police have done all they can, but occasionally, there are those who are unsatisfied, don't trust the police, or just can't wait. That's when Lincoln Investigations often got a call.

"I'm sure they're doing everything they can to find him," Annie said.

"Perhaps they are," Mr. White said. "But there're only two detectives on the case and I don't feel confident." He paused. "Can you help me?"

"Was the detective you talked to named Hank Corning?"

"Yes. Detective Hank Corning. That's what his card says."

"He's very capable," Annie said. "My husband and I have known him a long time."

"Nonetheless, can you help me? Are you too busy?"

Lincoln Investigations had nothing pressing at the moment, but she didn't want to interfere when she knew Hank would have everything under control.

She hesitated, then said, "We'll come and see you before we decide." She jotted down Mr. White's address, looked at her watch, and agreed to meet him at home by 2:30 that afternoon.

She told Jake about the call, then hurried out the door, making it to the cafe a few minutes late. Mrs. McKinley sat at a table on a small patio out front and Annie sat opposite her, declining her invitation for a drink.

"I'm afraid your suspicions were correct," Annie said, pushing the envelope toward her.

Mrs. McKinley opened the envelope and removed the photos, running through them slowly. Her face grew sadder with each shot. When she finished, she sighed and looked at Annie. "Thank you," she said, her voice weak and lifeless.

"I'm sorry," Annie said. "It must be hard."

Mrs. McKinley smiled feebly. "Now I have to decide what to do with these."

"The video is more of the same," Annie said.

The woman nodded and tucked the photos back into the envelope.

"It didn't take us more than a few hours," Annie said. "I'll give you a refund for the extra."

Mrs. McKinley shook her head. "You earned it."

"Are you sure?"

"Yes." She picked up her small Prada handbag and removed a twenty, tucked it under her coffee cup, then stood and picked up the envelope. "I have an appointment," she said. "I must go. Thank you again."

Annie watched her leave, wondering what would become of the woman's marriage. Whether they got divorced or not, she was afraid Mrs. McKinley was in for some more heartache, and all the money in the world couldn't heal a broken heart.

Annie called Jake and told him she was on her way back, and he promised to meet her outside. He was sitting on the curb when she pulled up and he hopped in.

On the way to Teddy White's house, she filled him in on her meeting with Mrs. McKinley. He didn't say much, but Annie could tell Jake felt sympathetic toward the woman.

The White residence was a beautiful, well-kept home in a middle-class subdivision. The immaculate lawn was framed by an abundance of flowers and colorful shrubs. Still more lined the front of the house and ran along the pathway toward the front door.

Jake rang the bell and waited. The man who answered the door a few moments later forced a weak smile, and after introductions, invited them into the front room.

Jake sat on one end of the couch, Annie the other. She glanced around the pristine room, sparsely furnished with modern furniture, everything in its place and neatly arranged. A huge spray of fresh flowers filled a vase on the coffee table, another on a stand by the doorway. It gave the room a beautiful smell unmatched by artificial sprays and deodorizers.

Mr. White dropped into a straight-backed chair with a sigh and leaned forward slightly. The smile had been replaced by a downcast expression, his voice quivering as he told them about his wife and how she had been killed. He paused often to look down and regain his composure before he was finished.

Annie had a notepad out and she wrote down the important points. "You said you knew the name of the suspect?" she asked.

Mr. White's lips tightened, anger in his eyes. "Adam Thorburn," he said, almost spitting the name out. "And he's run off somewhere. His mother, Virginia Thorburn, claims not to know where he is."

"And you want us to help look for him?" Jake asked.

Mr. White nodded, his brow wrinkled. "Yes. I want him found. He's a maniac, and if he hurts someone else, I couldn't live with myself if I hadn't done everything possible to stop him."

Annie watched the despondent man a moment as he wrung his hands, his shoulders slumped, pleading to them with his eyes. She looked at Jake. He nodded slightly and she turned back to Mr. White.

"We'll look into it," she said.

Teddy sat back and took a deep breath, letting it out slowly, a look of relief on his thin face. "Thank you. I expect you can reach me here at any time. I don't have plans to go out in the near future." He dropped his head. "At least, not until they release my wife's body."

"I'll keep you up to date," Annie said. She hesitated, watched the mournful man, then added, "The police department offers a grief counseling service if you're interested."

Mr. White nodded and didn't answer. He stood. "I assume you'll need a retainer."

Jake nodded, stood, and followed the man to a small office.

Annie rose from the couch and went to the fireplace. She glanced at a recent picture of the smiling couple and another one taken many years before on their wedding day. They looked as happy together in the recent one as they had back then, and her heart broke for the despairing new widower.

The two men returned and Jake handed her a check. She tucked it into her handbag along with her notepad and turned to the grieving man. "We'll look into this immediately. Please call if you have anything else that might help us."

Mr. White promised he would, then thanked them and saw them out.

They went to the car and got in. Jake turned to Annie as she started the car. "Where do we begin with this one?"

"I think we'll have to give Virginia Thorburn a visit," Annie said. "It seems like the only logical place to start."

CHAPTER 12

Tuesday, 2:44 p.m.

ADAM THORBURN walked with slumped shoulders, plodding down the sidewalk toward the place he had always called his home. His long afternoon walk had helped clear his head as he fought to make sense of his illness and why he was cursed with an unstable mind. Though he didn't make any headway in understanding himself, he was more optimistic, ready to face another weary day.

Most of the time, he was perfectly fine and able to function like anyone else. But at other times he heard voices and saw things that didn't exist. That's what held him back and convinced him he would never be like the rest. Life had thrown him a curve ball and it sucked to be him.

He kicked at a soda can, sending it whirling into the street. A squirrel raised its head and was gone, frightened into a tree, darting away from an imagined threat. That's what he was—an imagined threat, outcast and shunned. But after last night's events, he feared he was no longer harmless—he was dangerous.

He stopped short and ducked behind a tree. It was unusual for outsiders to visit this neighborhood, and even more peculiar for anyone to park along the street when most driveways had parking space to spare for any visitors who might happen by. And the vehicle parked in front of his house was unusual indeed.

An unmoving figure sat in the driver seat and Adam waited. The person remained still, like they were watching, waiting. Were they waiting for him?

He glanced toward the house. His mother's car was gone. She must've left already, but that didn't make a lot of sense. She wanted him to fix up the fender of the car first. And it wouldn't be in the garage; there was too much junk in there. Perhaps she had driven the vehicle the way it was; he had been away awhile.

Or maybe he was being paranoid again. He often found it difficult to separate his unwarranted paranoia from reality.

He stepped from his hiding place, then ducked back quickly. He saw his mother through the kitchen window above the sink, doing dishes, or cleaning up.

So where was the car? Something didn't make sense. Perhaps he'd caused some damage to another vehicle during the accident and they had tracked him down. They must be waiting for him to return. That was the only answer.

He turned and dashed back down the street a short distance, cut across an empty lot, then crossed the neighbor's back lawn. He would approach his house from the rear, then go in the back door and talk to his mother. He needed to find out what was going on before he came clean and gave himself up.

He dropped over a scraggy shrub, ducked behind the garage, and peered toward the road. He couldn't see the visitor's car from here, and that meant the watcher couldn't see him.

Streaking across the lawn, he climbed onto the small porch by the back door. The spring sang as he pulled open the screen door. He twisted the knob; the door was locked. He tapped gently and peeked through the window leading into the mudroom.

In a moment, his mother appeared, her eyes widening when she saw his face. She raised a finger to her lips in silence, then glanced behind her and crept to the door.

She eased it open carefully, quietly, and he moved back as she stepped out onto the back porch, closing the door gently behind her.

"They're waiting for you," she whispered.

He stared at his mother a moment, unsure what to say, then, "I saw a car at the road."

She touched his shoulder and leaned in. "There's a cop in the house too. It's not safe."

"Where's your car?" he asked.

"They took it away. They said it's evidence."

"Evidence? What's this all about?" he asked, confused, afraid, his paranoia growing.

His mother glanced toward the door, then turned back and put a hand on each of his shoulders. She leaned in close, her eyes anxious as she gazed into his. "They said ..." She paused and stood straight. "They said you killed a woman."

His eyes widened, his mouth fell open, and he took a sharp breath, unable to move or think.

"You can't stay here," she said.

Adam found his voice. "But how? Why? Why would I kill anyone?"

"It must've been an accident," she said, glancing toward the door. "They said you ran over her."

"If it was an accident ... then it's not my fault."

She whispered, "They said murder. They said you did it on purpose and they came for you." Her face flushed with anger. "They had a warrant and they searched the house and took the car."

"But I wouldn't—"

His mother put her arms around him, rocking him gently back and forth. He felt her breath in his ear, and she spoke in a soothing voice. "I know you wouldn't do it on purpose, but you weren't in your right mind."

More paranoia, along with panic and desperation, gripped his mind. He hated violence and would never hurt anyone. But this wasn't the first time he'd done something so out of character, nor the first time someone had witnessed his ferocious antics and turned him in. And each time, the solution had been to change his medication and the madness had subsided. For a while.

"You have to leave here," his mother said.

"Where … where'll I go? I have no place to go."

"I don't know," she said. "I'll think of something later, but right now, it's not safe here. If they put you in prison, you'll die there. They won't help you." She moved back, her hands on his shoulders, and shook him gently. "You have to go."

He nodded. "I … I'll find somewhere to hide."

"Maybe you can come back later. They can't stay here forever and wait for you." She held up a finger. "Stay here. I'll be back in a minute." She stepped inside quietly, easing the door closed behind her.

He waited on the porch, glancing fearfully around. His mind was spinning out of control, and he found it hard to think, feeling agitated, filled with terror of the unknown—terror of the future.

This was the first time he had actually hurt anyone and he was afraid, unsure what to do. No one seemed to understand him. No one even cared enough to try to understand.

At the last visit to the shrink, the doctor had informed him there were no new medications to try. At first they seemed to work, but he slowly deteriorated into madness—a madness that had now resulted in the death of an innocent woman.

The door opened again and his mother stepped out, a plastic grocery bag in one hand. She handed it to him. "There's some food in here. Enough for a couple of days. And your meds are in here too. Make sure you take them every day."

He looked into her eyes, frantically seeking answers, where to go, what to do. There was no response from her troubled eyes, no solution on her worried face.

"Go now," she said.

Adam took one last look into the uneasy eyes of the woman who took care of him. The woman who was there after his father died, and the woman he might never see again. One last fearful look, then he turned and shuffled across the lawn, disappearing behind the garage, back the way he'd come.

He was alone in an uncaring world with only his unstable mind to guide him.

There was no one he could depend on anymore. Not even himself.

CHAPTER 13

Tuesday, 3:21 p.m.

JAKE SAT AT THE desk in the office, browsing MapQuest to find the exact location of Virginia Thorburn's house. He printed out a map of the area surrounding 112 Mill Street, folded it, and tucked it into his pocket.

Matty poked his head in the doorway. "I'm home, Dad. Where's Mom?"

Jake pushed back his chair and looked at his son. "We have to go out for a little while. Your mother ran next door to see if Chrissy will watch you."

"No problem," Matty said. "Kyle and I have stuff to do anyway."

The back door opened and closed.

"It sounds like she's back now," Jake said as he stood, heading for the kitchen. "We won't be gone long."

"No problem," Annie said when Jake entered the room. "Chrissy'll watch him. Are you ready?"

"Ready," Jake said.

Matty said goodbye and ran out the back door.

Annie got her handbag from the counter and followed Jake outside, and they got into the car. Earlier, she had looked up Virginia Thorburn's phone number and called her under the pretense of a sales call, finding out the woman would be home until 5:00. That gave them lots of time.

Jake started the car, pulled from the driveway, and glanced at Annie. "I'm not sure how receptive Mrs. Thorburn will be to a visit from us. Her son is accused of murder and she might be on the defensive."

"We'll have to tread lightly," Annie said thoughtfully, buckling her seat belt.

Jake pulled out the map, consulted it, then handed it to Annie. "They're right on the edge of town," he said. "The only thing further north is the steel mill, and then on the other side of the tracks, it's all government property. Forest, swamp, and some vacant land."

A few minutes later, Jake pulled onto Mill Street, a narrow two-lane road of crumbling asphalt. A sidewalk ran along the right side, mature trees overhanging the roadway.

"There it is," Annie said, pointing ahead and to her right. "Number 112."

Jake slowed and squinted at the numbers displayed beside the front door. He glanced to his left. A car sat directly across the road from the house, a lone figure visible in the driver seat. Jake pulled to the shoulder and turned off the engine.

Annie gazed at the parked vehicle. "I think he's watching for Adam," she said, climbing from the car. "I'll be right back."

She crossed the road, went around the car, and tapped on the window. She leaned down and talked to the driver. Jake got out of the Firebird when Annie returned.

"It's Officer Spiegle," she said. "Another officer's in the house in case Adam returns. There're cops all over the city looking for him."

"They have a better chance of finding him than we do," Jake said.

"We'll do our best," Annie said, stepping onto the sidewalk, Jake following. They went up the gravel driveway to the side of the house.

Annie opened a tattered screen door and tapped on the inner door. They waited.

The door scraped open and a woman appeared, giving an impatient sigh. "Yes?"

"Virginia Thorburn?" Annie asked with a pleasant smile.

"Yes."

Annie introduced them and said, "We're concerned about Adam, and we'd like to help him if we can."

Jake wasn't sure how true that was, but he would go along with Annie's story.

"How can you help him?" the woman asked with a frown, dropping one hand to her hip.

"Perhaps we could come in and talk?" Annie said.

Mrs. Thorburn hesitated, then sighed again and moved back, waving them in. "You might as well join the circus. Everybody else is."

Annie and Jake stepped through the doorway into the stale-smelling kitchen, the screen door slapping closed behind them. The woman sat at the table and crossed her legs, tugging her short, tight skirt into place. She puffed at a lit cigarette, then took a sip of coffee from a stained mug, eyeing them over the top.

"Might as well sit down," she said.

The Lincolns pulled back chairs and sat facing the woman.

She took a long drag of her lipstick-stained cigarette and blew the smoke at the ceiling. "I don't know how you can help Adam, but I'm willing to listen."

"Mrs. Thorburn," Annie began, then hesitated. "We know Adam is accused of killing a woman, and the police are claiming they have evidence against him."

The woman cocked her head. "Who'd you say hired you?"

Annie answered slowly, "We've been retained by the husband of the victim—"

Jake interrupted, glancing at Annie. "But we're only interested in the truth. Nothing more." He leaned in and looked intently at Mrs. Thorburn. "If Adam is innocent, then we want to prove it."

Annie nodded. "We were hoping you could help us, and in turn, help your son."

"Help how? I don't know if he did it or not, and neither does he."

Jake frowned. "How can he not know?"

She butted her smoke out and took the last sip of her coffee. "Because Adam is schizophrenic. He doesn't always remember what he does."

Jake glanced at Annie. He didn't know much about schizophrenia and he wasn't sure Annie did either.

"He has blackout periods sometimes," Mrs. Thorburn said, dropping her eyes. "I'm afraid he's guilty." She paused a moment, then looked up and added quickly, earnestly, her voice shaking, "But he didn't do it on purpose. Never. Never."

Annie spoke softly. "Do you know where Adam is, Mrs. Thorburn?"

She shook her head. "I have no idea."

"Does he go away often?"

"No. But after last night …" Her voice trailed off and she took an uneasy breath. "If he remembers what he did, he might not come back."

"Could he be at a friend's house?" Jake asked.

She shook her head slowly. "He has no friends."

Annie leaned in and touched the woman's trembling hand. "Any relatives?"

"Not in this part of the country. Maybe out East. I don't know. My husband never mentioned any family."

"Where's your husband?" Annie asked.

Mrs. Thorburn's mascara ran as a few tears escaped her downcast eyes. "Died. Almost a year ago. Left me with this place and Adam."

"I'm sorry."

Mrs. Thorburn plucked a tissue from a box on the table

and dabbed at the tears, smearing her makeup. She took a shaky breath and looked away. "He wasn't much good anyway."

Jake studied the distraught woman. She looked like she'd lived a rough life. She'd lost her husband and would soon lose her son. And with no family to turn to, things could only get worse.

Mrs. Thorburn looked back and forth between Jake and Annie. "Adam's an honest boy. If he's convinced he's guilty, he might turn himself in eventually. The only thing is ..." Her voice trailed off, her lower lip quivering.

Annie spoke soothingly. "Yes?"

The woman pulled her hand back and dropped it into her lap, clasping her hands together. "I might never see him again. He's actually quite timid, and he would be afraid to go to prison."

Jake leaned forward. "Then we have to find him as soon as possible."

Mrs. Thorburn lit another cigarette and took a couple of long drags. It seemed to calm her and she leaned in. "It might be best to leave him be. Let him make up his own mind what to do." She dabbed at her eyes. "I'm sure he'll do the right thing. I only want him to be safe."

"So do we, Mrs. Thorburn," Annie said. "So do we."

CHAPTER 14

Tuesday, 3:44 p.m.

HANK RECEIVED a call from lead crime scene investigator Rod Jameson. The final report on the murder of Nina White was ready and waiting on Hank's desk.

He had been interviewing neighbors of the Thorburns at the time of the call—necessary and tedious work that had to be done. Often it turned up a lead, but today he'd received little information about Adam Thorburn. Few in the neighborhood knew him all that well. He was described as a quiet boy, and seemed to be a loner.

In addition to issuing the BOLO on Thorburn, Hank had officers canvassing the entire neighborhood. Houses in all directions were being visited in the hopes someone either had seen Adam Thorburn or could supply information as to his whereabouts. To this point, no one could furnish a lead, and many didn't know the boy or the Thorburns.

It didn't look promising.

He returned to the precinct, went to his desk and sat, pulling in his chair. He picked up the forensics report and browsed the paperwork. After thoroughly examining the evidence and accompanying photographs, Hank saw no surprises in the conclusions drawn by the investigators. Their work served to confirm Hank's assumptions about what had gone on in the parking lot late last evening.

The impounded vehicle had been inspected, and the report concluded the tire track found at the scene of the murder was from the same car. Furthermore, the lab ascertained the blood found between the treads of the tire was of the same group as Nina White's blood.

The paint from the vehicle was also compared to chips found on Nina White's car, and along with photos, they concluded the damage was caused by the vehicle in question. A search of Nina's car had turned up nothing of further interest.

A fine powdering of glass was also found in the grill and on the hood of the vehicle. Forensics couldn't ascertain whether or not it came from Nina White's car, only that it was consistent, but Hank had no question about it.

A botanical expert was consulted, and he affirmed the rose found in the mouth of the victim was the same species as the ones which grew along the rear wall of the Thorburn house.

The search of the Thorburn residence turned up nothing

incriminating and contained no clues as to where Adam Thorburn might be hiding out.

His cell phone rang and he answered it. It was Teddy White—again.

"Detective, do you have any news for me?"

Hank held his patience. "Nothing yet, Mr. White. You need to allow more time. Adam Thorburn is on the run and we'll track him down, but at this point, we don't know where he is."

"I've hired some private investigators," Mr. White said.

Hank frowned at his phone. There were several PIs in this town and he didn't want any of them mucking around with the evidence and getting in the way of a police investigation. "That's well within your rights," Hank said. "But it might be a little premature."

"The Lincolns promised they would help."

Hank's vision of an interfering gumshoe vanished. There were none so thorough and as caring as his good friends, Jake and Annie Lincoln, who were always careful to stay out of the way of law enforcement. He had worked alongside them in the past, helping him to crack some tough cases. And though Captain Diego rarely admitted it outwardly, they often had his unwritten blessing.

"Mr. White," Hank said, "I'll call you as soon as we have anything concrete." He didn't want to give the grieving widower the brush-off, but he needed to be firm. "I'll inform you the minute we find the suspect."

"Very well. I'll call you again tomorrow. Thank you, Detective."

Hank hung up. He always felt deeply for the victims, and he sympathized with Teddy White. Though he had never personally experienced the loss of a loved one at the hands of a violent killer, he'd seen enough heartache and senseless murders as head of RHPD Robbery/Homicide to do him a lifetime.

He was a little surprised the Lincolns hadn't called him regarding their involvement, so he dialed Jake's number.

"We just got back," Jake explained. "I haven't have a chance to let you know yet."

"I'll drop by and see you guys after work," Hank said. "It's been a while."

"We'll fill you in on our visit to Virginia Thorburn while you're here."

Hank hung up and glanced toward Detective King's desk. He didn't expect to see King for a while. Hank had him organizing the neighborhood search for Adam Thorburn, and it could easily take him the rest of the day.

He looked up as the front desk officer approached and handed him an envelope. A scrawl on the front revealed it was from Richmond North High School.

Hank dumped its contents onto his desk. It was a five-page report on Adam Thorburn, retrieved from the school's record storage. Hank leafed through it. The neatly stapled report contained Adam's vital information along with Nina White's handwritten notes on her meetings with the student.

Among other things, the report showed Adam had barely made passing grades during the two years he attended Richmond North High School. Those grades were inconsistent with his above-average IQ of 130. In her notes, Nina attributed his poor grades to a lack of applying himself. It was noted Adam was schizophrenic but rarely showed negative signs at school.

But that was all seven years ago, and according to his mother, his condition had deteriorated since then.

During Adam's counseling sessions with Mrs. White, her notes showed she had attempted to encourage him but had been unable to impress on him the importance of a good education. He had seemed distracted and had been easily discouraged. She'd made note of his occasional comments regarding the bullying he received from other students.

At Mrs. White's request to interview Adam's parents, Adam's mother had attended several meetings with her over the two years. His father hadn't bothered to show up for any of the appointments. It was noted at the final meeting that, in Mrs. White's opinion, his home life was less than ideal and might be a detriment to his desire to learn. There were no details as to exactly what she meant by this opinion.

Hank put the report aside. He had a good idea what Adam's home life must've been like. The Thorburns lived on the edge of poverty, which was no excuse to commit murder, but it wasn't an environment that would foster a lot of motivation to succeed. He wondered what would've turned the quiet boy into a vicious murderer.

He glanced across the room when he heard his name called. Captain Diego stood in the door of his office, waving him over. Hank stood, went into Diego's office, and took a seat.

Diego sat forward, rested his arms on his desk, and looked at Hank. "Anything positive on the Nina White murder yet?"

"Lots of positive," Hank said. "We have a solid suspect. We just can't locate him."

As Hank went over the evidence with Diego, the captain brushed at his dark mustache with two fingers, listening intently.

When Hank was done, Diego sat back, a frown on his round face. "I'll give you all the support you need on this, Hank. Whatever you want. Just find the guy."

"I'm doing my best, Captain. We'll get him."

"Keep me informed." Diego dismissed him with a wave and went back to his paperwork.

Hank returned to his desk and called King, but the detective wasn't having any luck. "It doesn't look like he's hanging around the neighborhood. Nobody's seen him."

"Keep at it," Hank said and hung up. It was doubtful Adam Thorburn had much money or food. He would have to surface eventually, and Hank wanted to be there when he did.

CHAPTER 15

Tuesday, 4:29 p.m.

ADAM EASED DOWN onto the rough floorboards and laid his head back against the wall. He would be safe here for now, but how long could he last with no food and nothing but a tumbledown shack in the swamp for shelter?

He might be able to pick some wild berries or apples that grew along the edge of the wetlands, but it would hardly be enough to nourish him. And when the cold came, the swamp would sleep until spring, and he couldn't survive without a constant source of food and heat.

The heat he could take care of. There were enough dead and dying trees in the area to furnish him with fuel, and he could insulate the hut with grass or straw hauled from a farmer's field a mile or so away. He could survive the winter without fear of freezing to death, but food was his main concern. The small wildlife in the area would all but disappear in the winter, and even if he could trap the occasional rabbit, meat of any kind would be scarce.

He had some life-and-death decisions to make and there was no one else he could turn to.

But winter was still a long way off, and it was impossible to tell what might happen to him in the meantime. For all he knew, and sometimes for all he cared, he could be dead by then. That might be for the best anyway. He was a burden on society, a burden on his mother, and always a burden to himself.

He glanced around the single-room hut. He had discovered this place many years ago and enjoyed some peaceful times here—away from the rest of the cruel and uncaring world, and away from his parents' arguing. He hadn't been here since his father had died, and he'd kept this place a secret. It was a safe haven, and a place where he could be alone and not have to hear about what a loser he was.

But back then, he'd known he could always return home after he'd recharged his soul. Now, this was home, and there was no turning back.

He sighed and turned his eyes toward the ceiling. The roof was still intact, and the walls, although leaning and bulging in places, still appeared solid enough. Whoever had built this place had done a good job, considering the location. He wondered what it had been used for at the time. Perhaps it was once someone's home. Maybe someone who needed a refuge—just like him.

The shack was dry, built on a solid piece of land rising above the swampy waters, and the builder had mounted it on half a dozen firm wooden pillars to be certain it would endure. That kept it well above the rising and falling of the waters.

Unlike most people who shunned the muddy, decaying wetland, looking on it as nothing more than a place to be feared, a place of death and decay, Adam felt at home in the steaming bog. Much like himself, it was misunderstood. It was a place of vibrant life and rebirth, a place of new beginnings and innocence.

He closed his eyes and breathed in the pungent odor surrounding him. The beautiful fragrance of constantly decaying vegetation signified a second chance. The black waters of the wild wetland would regenerate, sprout anew, and breathe fresh life into death.

If it were possible, he would throw himself into the beautiful black waters and reincarnate into what he yearned to be—normal, like the rest of the world, happy, healthy, and free.

A bullfrog's deep voice spoke somewhere close by. Adam opened his eyes and gazed through the small window—a square hole in the wall—and strained to see the visitor. The thick foliage and the rising steam perfectly camouflaged the creature from its predators, invisible to all but a mate perhaps waiting nearby.

The situation he found himself in was completely beyond

his control. His illness had caused him to do the unthinkable—take the life of another human being. Though the voices in his head hadn't presented themselves today, he knew they would be back. It was only a matter of time before they hounded him again, causing him to make another rash move.

He wondered how many times he'd hurt someone, or worse still, killed another human being without knowing it. The woman might not have been the first—just the first time he got caught.

If worse came to worst, he would allow himself to die in the swamp rather than let the voices control him. The problem was, when he blacked out he didn't know what he did. He could kill someone and never know it had happened.

It was a despairing thought, and he felt helpless. There was nothing he could do about it, and it all seemed to be beyond the expertise of his doctor, the doctor he might never see again. Dr. Zalora would turn him in for sure. Even his mother wouldn't be able to help him much. The police would be certain to keep an eye on the house in case he returned, and the penalty for sheltering a fugitive from justice would be more than she deserved.

He rose wearily to his feet and stepped outside the hut. On the high ground where he stood, weeds and wildflowers thrived. Vines swallowed one side of the building, reaching for the sun from the rooftop. Lush grass flourished in patches of dark green about his feet. Here and there an evergreen stood amid the quaking moss. Tall reeds shot upwards from the muddy ground a few feet away, and further down, the swamp bubbled and steamed endlessly.

Adam wondered if they would track him here. They would scour the neighborhood and perhaps the rest of the city, but surely no one would think he had retreated to such a desolate and dangerous place. Maybe they would give up eventually, assuming he'd moved from the city, or maybe even out of the country.

That is, if he could keep himself under control and not make an appearance during one of his blackout periods.

Perhaps he was being too optimistic, a rather unusual state for him. He was more used to being unduly paranoid, in fear of the unknown, frightened of unseen dangers that permeated his thoughts and overwhelmed him with panic.

It was during those irrational panic attacks he entertained thoughts of ending it all. He often found himself on the cusp of a decision—to give in entirely to the voices, or stop them forever by ending his own worthless existence.

He never seemed to make that decision. During those times when his will was weak, perhaps it was a natural instinct for self-preservation that aided him in the battle against the voices. When the panic subsided, he still existed as before. Nothing changed.

Long ago, he had given up hope they would ever find a cure. His case was unusual, the doctor told him. His advice was to adapt, persevere, and hope one day ongoing research would result in something to stabilize him. All he wanted was to get his life back and be normal. Was that too much to hope for?

Adam sat down on a rock by the edge of the teeming bog,

pulled his feet up, and wrapped his arms around his legs. He gazed over the landscape in front of him, swamp as far as he could see, the place he now called home. It would take care of him, feed his soul, and nourish his mind, and the small measure of peace it brought to his tortured heart would be all he could hope for.

CHAPTER 16

Tuesday, 6:18 p.m.

ANNIE SAT IN her favorite chair in the living room, her legs curled underneath her, staring unseeing at the television. It was the first time they'd taken on a murder case that was already solved. The police were on the hunt for a solid suspect, and it was just a matter of time before they brought the killer in.

With their limited resources, she was unsure how she and Jake could aid in the hunt for Adam Thorburn. The police had employed their manpower to exhaust all possible leads, yet they had been unable to find information pointing to his whereabouts.

She glanced down at Matty. He lay on his back, a cushion

under his head, absorbed in a comic book. Jake was on the couch, stretched out, his hands behind his head. He seemed to be in thought, his eyes on the ceiling rather than the muted television.

He swung his feet to the floor, sat up and leaned forward, looking at Annie. "I think Virginia Thorburn knows more than she's telling us," he said.

Annie glanced at Jake. "What makes you say that?"

"It was something she said before we left, that she thought it best to leave Adam alone and let him make up his own mind. I think she might know where he is, but she doesn't want to turn him in against his will."

Annie thought about Jake's statement, then asked, "But if she knows, how do we get that information from her?"

Jake shrugged. "I have no idea, but if she's covering for him, he might show up at the house again."

"The police are watching the house."

"True enough," Jake said. "But she knows that. She might meet him elsewhere."

"So you think we should tail her?"

Jake sat back and shrugged one shoulder. "Just a thought. I'm trying to come up with some ideas."

The doorbell rang and Matty dropped his comic, sprang to his feet, and ran to the door. A moment later, Hank's voice came from the foyer. "Hey, Matty."

"Hey, Uncle Hank."

The cop followed Matty into the living room, set his briefcase on the floor, and sat on the other end of the couch. Matty dropped in between Hank and his father.

"I assume you didn't find Adam Thorburn yet?" Jake asked.

Hank shook his head. "Not yet, but as soon as he shows his face, we'll get him. He has to come out of hiding some time."

"They showed a photo of him on the news," Annie said. "The whole town must know what he looks like by now."

"And Teddy White thinks we can help," Jake said. "He was almost begging us. We took the case, but we don't know where to start."

"If we don't find Adam right away, it's just a matter of time," Hank said. "He's on medication to control his schizophrenia. Assuming he has it with him, he'll run out eventually and have to find more or he'll be unstable."

Annie looked at Matty. Her son was intent on the conversation, his eyes moving back and forth between Hank and Jake. She often let him listen in, but when things turned to more gruesome matters, she would rather he didn't hear.

"Matty, will you go to your room for now?" she asked.

Matty frowned. "What did I do, Mom?"

"Nothing. It's just for a few minutes." She pointed to the doorway. "Read a book or something for now."

"Aw, Mom." Matty slid off the couch and picked up his comic book. He turned to Hank and faked a pout. "Bye, Uncle Hank."

Hank leaned forward for a fist bump. "See you, Matty."

The boy frowned at his mother, then turned and sauntered away, slowly thumping up the stairs.

Annie leaned forward and looked at Hank. "When Adam

runs out of medication, he might kill again. If he's already unstable with his medication, how much worse will he be without it?"

"That's exactly what I'm afraid of," Hank said. "The murder of Nina White was so cold-blooded and brutal, the next one might be as horrendous." He picked up his briefcase, laid it in his lap, and flipped it open. He pulled out a business card and studied it. "I dropped by to see Adam's psychiatrist this afternoon. Dr. Zalora. He was shocked when he heard the news, but not surprised. He expressed concern Adam had deteriorated lately and they were running out of medical options to stabilize his behavior."

"They've tried everything?" Annie asked.

"Not everything," Hank said. "There're some more aggressive medications, but they're new and very expensive. It's a question of money as well. Mrs. Thorburn has limited funds, and there's no government assistance available for the medication."

"So either way, his actions are completely out of control," Jake said.

Hank closed his briefcase, sat it on the floor, and leaned back. "Not completely. Nina White wasn't a random victim. There was some level of planning on Adam's part. He knew the victim, and if she was targeted, he had to have known how to find her."

"Perhaps his gripe was with the school," Annie said. "Maybe he would've killed the first person who came along."

"That's a possibility," Hank said. "But it's certain he planned to kill someone." He paused. "The ME found a rose in the victim's mouth. The same roses that grow on the Thorburn property."

Annie frowned. "A rose?"

"It sounds like planning to me," Jake said.

Hank looked at Jake. "But not careful planning. He was careless about leaving evidence behind. He didn't worry about hiding the car or even covering his face." Hank shook his head slowly. "It's as if he didn't care about getting caught."

"Which tells me his mind is unstable," Annie said. "His only desire was to kill and never mind the consequences."

"Sounds more like a psychopath to me," Jake said.

"Perhaps," Hank said. "But according to his doctor, he's never displayed such extreme violence before. In the past, it was usually abnormal behavior, the occasional tantrum, or irrational anger."

"But the doctor said his behavior has deteriorated lately," Annie said.

Hank nodded. "And now he's completely out of control."

"What's the significance of the rose?" Jake asked.

"That's what I'm trying to figure out," Hank said. "It obviously has some meaning to him."

"What color was the rose?" Annie asked.

"Red."

"Love."

"That's what King suggested," Hank said. "Perhaps Adam was secretly in love with Nina White. She was a school guidance counselor, and a role like that tends to be more personal, almost like a therapist. It's not unusual for someone to fall in love, and even expect a relationship, with someone in that position."

"A therapist is focused entirely on you and your needs. What can be more gratifying than that?" Jake added.

"Exactly," Hank said. "And when a person is weak and unstable to start with, they might interpret it as signs of true caring and affection."

"But this was all years ago," Annie said.

"He might've buried his feelings all these years and they finally surfaced."

"Has Adam ever had a girlfriend?" Jake asked.

Hank shook his head. "I don't believe so. Apparently, he has no friends, was bullied at school, and keeps mostly to himself."

"Sounds like a recipe for disaster," Jake said.

"Add schizophrenia to the mix and that's exactly what you have," Hank said.

Jake sat back and scratched his head. "So, if Adam had a thing for Nina White, then she wasn't a random victim."

Hank nodded. "That's the presumption we're going with. The connection between Adam and Nina White is too solid to suggest otherwise."

"Then we have to hope she's his only victim," Annie said. "And he needs to be tracked down before we find out otherwise."

CHAPTER 17

Tuesday, 8:44 p.m.

RAYMOND RONSON pulled his 2004 Volkswagen Beetle up to the rear door of Millfield Elementary School and shut down the engine. After almost thirty years at the same job, a job he never tired of, he treated this place as his home away from home.

The kids he ran into during the day were like family. Sure, they came and went as they grew up and graduated to higher education, but there was always a nice assortment of youngsters who took the time to say hi when they saw him in the halls. And they enjoyed the stories he sometimes told. Short stories—enough to make them smile, but not too long to keep them from their studies.

He was here every school day until the kids went home, and the children were what made this job most enjoyable. He and Eunice hadn't been able to have any family of their own, and he was thankful for the day he'd found this job. It didn't pay a lot, but he and his wife had simple tastes and got by nicely.

And cleaning up after kids was a joy—part of the job, and he wouldn't trade what he did for twice the money. Each evening, when he popped back to do a final cleaning after the staff cleared out, he took pride in making the place sparkle, all clean and shiny, ready for the kids on the next school day.

Picking up his cap from the passenger seat, Raymond sat it on his head and worked it into place. He brushed back the hair above his ears, just enough hair that no one would suspect he had an expanding bald spot under the cap. Not that he cared. There was no shame in being bald.

He stepped from the car, each day growing more mindful of the increasing effort it took him to get around. At sixty-eight, he had a lot of good years left, but he felt his age creeping up on him. But never mind—complaining never did any good, and anyway, his job wasn't all that back-breaking.

Stepping to the rear door, he tugged at the key ring fastened to his belt with a chain, selected a key, and unlocked the door. He heaved on the handle and the door scraped open. The bottom brushed the concrete and held. He would have to get around to fixing that up soon. It was probably the hinges sagging. He could tighten it up with a screwdriver, allowing the door to swing closed properly on its own.

He stepped into the dimly lit hallway and tugged at the

door to free it. It almost caught his heels as it scraped behind him and snapped closed. He flicked a light switch on the wall, flooding the hall with cool fluorescent light. One bulb flickered and would soon die. Maybe he would take care of that first. Bulbs didn't last forever. Except for him, people rarely came into this area of the building, but he needed the bright lighting for his own aging eyes.

Raymond shuffled down the hall, pushed open a metal door, and stepped into the supply room. He lugged an aluminum ladder out, stood it under the dying bulb, and carefully climbed the steps. Reaching up, he slipped the plastic light cover aside and twisted the bulb gently. It had been there awhile. One end was corroded and stubborn, but he tugged, and it finally moved.

The end of the forty-eight-inch tube slipped from his grasp and swung downward. He grabbed for it, missed, and watched in disgust as the bulb did a somersault, hit the hard tile floor, and exploded. He shook his head, annoyed at his own clumsiness, and climbed back down the ladder. He avoided tramping in the shattered glass as he pushed the ladder out of the way. He would sweep up the mess before he installed a new bulb.

He ambled down the corridor to the far end, pushing open a door that led into the main area of the building. To his left and right, lockers lined the hallway, classroom doors at even intervals along the far side. He squinted in the subdued lighting, moved to his left, and opened the storage room where he kept his organized array of cleaning supplies and equipment.

Flicking on the storage room light, he chose a wide push broom from the selection hanging on the wall and went back to the entrance corridor.

He opened the door and frowned. The light had gone out. That was strange because he knew he'd left it on. Anyway, the light switch was by the exit door at the other end of the long hallway and he didn't remember turning it off. Why would he?

Even more strange, the outside door was open. The roof of his car, parked outside, shone in the bright moonlight.

"Who's there?" he called, cupping a hand behind his ear, waiting for an answer.

No one did. He called again. "Hello? Is someone there?" He paused to listen, then headed for the exit, pushing the broom ahead of him.

Halfway down the corridor, he stopped short when a silhouette appeared in the doorway. Something wasn't right. A darkened figure stood straight, legs spread, arms out at the sides.

His dimming eyes could make out something gripped in one fist—something like the shape of a knife, but smaller, and pointed, maybe a screwdriver.

Raymond's voice came out uneasily as he stood still, cautiously observing the intruder. "Who're you? What do you want?"

There was no answer. Instead the figure took a slow step, shoulders hunched forward.

Raymond took a careful step backward, dragging the broom with him. Then another step as the figure came closer.

He heard feet crunching on broken glass. The intruder stopped a moment, then moved forward again. Slowly.

Raymond took one more step back, dropping the broom in his haste to get away. He was frightened now, determined not to stay there any longer.

He spun around and stumbled in the darkness, falling heavily against the wall. He righted himself and looked over his shoulder. The intruder was still coming. Faster now.

Raymond's breath labored with the effort, his heart pounding against his ribs, his eyes straining as he staggered toward the door leading into the main area of the school.

He knew of a place he might be able to hide, but first, he would have to get out of this corridor. He would have no chance of escape otherwise, with no chance of outrunning his stalker, and at his age, even less chance of overpowering anyone.

Footsteps quickened behind him, the intruder's breath almost in his ear.

Raymond panted as he hurried along, but his pace had slowed, and the door seemed so far away.

He would never make it.

Running was futile and he took the only choice he had. He turned around and faced his would-be attacker.

The unwelcome visitor stopped and Raymond's eyes widened in the darkness. He instinctively raised his hands for protection as the prowler lifted his arm. Raymond's terrified eyes saw the weapon clearly now. It was a screwdriver. Likely the one he would've used to fix the outer door.

His own screwdriver was about to be used as a weapon against him by a sadistic fiend.

100

Raymond's tortured mind asked why. Why, why?

The screwdriver descended, forcing its way into his chest. He gasped as the weapon was ripped free. His arms fell and he wavered, then he caught his balance, his eyes darkening.

He felt the deadly tool strike again. Felt it enter his body. Felt himself slip to the floor. He lay still, aware of breathing—not his own—as the killer crouched beside him. Then a hand on his chin, another on his nose, his jaw forced down. Something soft lay on his tongue.

Now fading footsteps, a door opened and closed, and he thought of Eunice, waiting for him at home. Dear, dear Eunice. The love of his life.

His pierced heart broke for her. She needed him, but he would never be there for her again.

CHAPTER 18

DAY 3 - Wednesday, 8:25 a.m.

ANNIE SAT HER coffee cup down, stood from the kitchen table, and answered a knock on the back door. It was Kyle, come to make his morning rendezvous with Matty before they headed off to school.

Annie pushed the door open and looked down at the grinning face. "Hi, Kyle. Matty's still upstairs."

"Thanks, Mrs. Lincoln," Kyle said, ducking under her arm and running toward the hallway.

Annie sat back down and picked up her cup. The boys would soon be off to school, Jake was in the shower, cooling off from his morning workout, and she had things to do.

The case had been on her mind throughout the night, and

she had plans to visit Mabel Shorn later in the day. She knew the Thorburns' neighbor didn't work and Annie hoped to catch her at home. Ed Shorn worked evenings, but her main concern was an interview with Virginia Thorburn's friend, Mabel.

She finished her drink, rinsed out her cup, removed Matty's lunch bag from the fridge, and leaned back against the counter. The boys laughed and giggled noisily as they clomped down the stairs and into the kitchen.

"Thanks, Mom," Matty said, grabbing the bag. He put it into his backpack, slung the pack over his shoulder, and kissed his mother as she leaned over, waiting.

"Bye, Mrs. Lincoln," Kyle said, following Matty from the room. She heard the murmur of Jake's voice in the front hallway, talking to the boys. Then the door slammed and Jake came into the kitchen, heading for the coffeepot.

Annie told him her plans as he fixed himself a drink and sat at the table. "I realize we're treading over ground Hank already covered," she said. "But we have no other leads. Besides, I like to hear things firsthand."

"I thought I might see if I can squeeze a few minutes from Adam Thorburn's shrink," Jake said. "He might know something he doesn't know he knows." He paused. "Besides, we have to earn our money."

Annie straightened her back. "I'll be in the office if you need me. I have a few things to do." She went to the office, sat down and pulled in her chair, booting up her iMac. She checked for phone messages while she waited. There were none.

The splash screen appeared on her monitor—a shot of Jake and Matty wrestling on the living room floor. She checked the email account for Lincoln Investigations, filtered through the spam and was left with one email. It had a curious subject line that caught her attention, "Help for your investigation."

She opened the email and leaned in. "Lincoln Investigations," it began. "If you want to know more about Adam Thorburn, come to Millfield Elementary School as soon as possible on Wednesday morning. Meet me inside the service door at the east side of the building. I'll be waiting."

There was no signature, but it was sent from Millfield Elementary School's main email address. Perhaps it was from one of the staff, or maybe even from a student. She checked the headers. Everything seemed normal as far as she could tell. She noted the email had been sent at 9:54 the previous evening. It wasn't likely from a student at that time of the evening.

It was a peculiar message and she wasn't sure how to handle it. Why had the sender contacted them via email rather than call? Sure, it was more anonymous, but once they met, all anonymity would be gone.

She looked at her watch. If they decided to go, they should go immediately.

She printed the email, carried it to the kitchen, sat down, and slid it in front of Jake. "What do you make of that?" she asked.

Jake set his coffee down, picked up the paper, and leaned back. He read the message, a frown growing on his face.

104

When he was finished he looked up. "Could be something," he said, laying the email on the table and looking at Annie. "We should check it out."

"Millfield Elementary School is close to the Thorburns'," Annie said. "It's the school Adam would have attended before high school."

Jake gulped the last of his coffee, stood, and put the cup in the sink. "Grab your bag of tricks," he said. "We might as well go right away."

Annie got her handbag, folded the email in two, and tucked it inside. She followed Jake out the front door and they got in the Firebird. Jake started the car and pulled onto the street, then turned to Annie, nodding toward her bag. "You have your recorder in there?"

"Always."

Fifteen minutes later, he turned the vehicle onto Mill Street and drove past the Thorburn house.

"It looks like the police have stopped watching for Adam to return," Annie said. "Their car's gone."

"I guess they can't sit there forever," Jake said. "Besides, it's doubtful Adam would come home. At least, not with a strange car sitting out front."

"They have a citywide lookout for him, anyway," Annie said, then pointed through the windshield. "The school's on the next street. Turn there."

Jake took a left turn, drove half a block, and turned into the school property. He drove through the parking lot toward the east side of the building and pulled into a slot beside a Volkswagen Beetle parked in front of the service entrance.

They got out, went around the Beetle, and approached the door. Jake pulled it open and peered into the dark corridor. Annie stepped around him and fumbled on the wall for a light switch. She found it and flicked it on, and the hallway flooded with light.

Her eyes widened and her mouth dropped open. Someone lay on the floor, halfway down the corridor, and he wasn't moving.

She moved forward cautiously a few steps, her breath quickening. Something crunched under her feet. There was glass on the floor—glass from a fluorescent bulb—and a ladder stood to one side. She looked up. It appeared someone had been changing a light bulb, and it had slipped and shattered on the floor.

Jake followed Annie as she skirted around the broken glass, stepped over a push broom lying on the floor, and stopped a few feet away from the unmoving body.

It was a man, an older man, and he lay on his back. There was a dark red patch of blood on his shirt and more on the floor. There was no doubt about it, the man was dead.

The eight-inch screwdriver protruding from his chest was the dead giveaway.

She turned back to Jake. He stood with his arms crossed, a deep frown on his face, staring down at the body.

"What did this guy do to deserve this?" he asked, giving a deep sigh.

"Nobody deserves this," Annie said.

"We'd better not go any closer. We don't want to disturb the evidence."

Annie turned her eyes back to the body. Was this the man who'd sent her an email claiming knowledge of Adam Thorburn? Or was the email sent by Adam, boasting to them about his latest victim?

She took a short step forward, crouched down, and peered. Something stuck out of the victim's mouth. It seemed to be a stem of a flower. Was it a rose? Was Adam taunting the police? Was he taunting them?

"I think there's a rose in his mouth," she said to Jake.

Jake's face was grim as he leaned forward and squinted. "It sure looks like it." He clenched his lips, his nostrils flared, and he shook his head slowly.

Annie looked at her watch. It was already past nine o'clock. School had begun, and yet no one had discovered the body. Perhaps none of the staff came to this area. But who was the man?

The email had been sent the previous evening, and by the look of the victim's clothes, this could be the janitor. He would've been here to do the cleaning, and the Beetle outside the door might be his car.

"I'll call the police," Jake said, pulling out his cell phone and moving toward the exit.

Annie followed him outside as Jake dialed 9-1-1.

CHAPTER 19

Wednesday, 9:18 a.m.

HANK PULLED into the parking lot at Millfield Elementary School, drove to the east side of the building, and stopped behind a police cruiser. The forensic van was parked nearby, investigators busy documenting the scene. An area outside the service entrance was taped off by the first responders, allowing CSI to do their work undisturbed.

Jake's Firebird was parked inside the secured area next to a Volkswagen Beetle. The Lincolns stood next to the vehicle, watching the proceedings. Uniformed officers held back the few onlookers who had discovered the situation and approached curiously.

Detective King pulled up in his vehicle, parked beside Hank, and strolled over. Hank got out of his car and greeted King with a nod, and together they walked past a waiting ambulance, ducking under the tape. Jake glanced over as they approached the Firebird.

"How on earth did you discover this one?" Hank asked, looking back and forth between Jake and Annie, a perplexed look on his face.

Annie rummaged in her bag and handed a folded paper to Hank. "I got this in my email box this morning," she said.

Hank read the message, gave it to King, then turned to Annie. "What did you guys make of the email?"

"I'm not sure if the victim sent it or the killer," Annie said. "If it was the victim, the killer must've known about the rendezvous. But if it was the killer, I assume he was taunting us."

King folded the paper and tucked it into his pocket.

"We'll figure it out," Hank said, and turned to King. "We'd better take a look inside." He reached into his jacket, pulled out two pairs of booties, and handed a pair to King. The detectives went to the entrance, stepped inside, and put the shoe coverings on.

Hank glanced down the long, narrow hallway, now a hub of activity. A CSI photographer was crouched beside the body, halfway down the corridor, his camera flashing. Beyond him, a doorway at the end of the hall was open.

Doorknobs and walls had been brushed for fingerprints, the floor tested for footprints.

Hank moved toward the body, carefully avoiding glass

shards littering an area a few feet inside the entrance. He stepped past an aluminum ladder that was pushed against the wall and approached lead investigator Rod Jameson.

"Morning, Rod," Hank said. "Do we know who the victim is yet?"

"Hey, Hank," Rod said, glancing at his clipboard. "The vic's name is Raymond Ronson, according to his driver's license. Sixty-eight years old." He cocked a thumb toward the exit door. "That's his Beetle outside. Registered in his name. According to one of the staff, he's the janitor here."

"Anything else you can tell us?" King asked.

"Not yet. A few prints. We're still trying to figure out exactly what went on here."

"Anything inside the main school area?"

"Not sure yet," Rod said. "But we've secured the entire building. Evacuated all the staff and students."

"Thanks, Rod," Hank said. He moved further down the hall, stopped in front of a broom laying haphazardly in the middle of the corridor, and pointed it out to King. "Looks like he was about to sweep up the glass."

Hank stepped over the broom and approached the body. He crouched down and gazed at the victim a moment. His blood boiled and he sighed deeply, remembering the victim had a name. It was Raymond Ronson, and he didn't deserve this.

He took a deep breath, pushed his feelings aside, and leaned in, peering closely at the screwdriver. It protruded from the dead man's chest, the shirt surrounding the area soaked with crimson.

King crouched beside Hank and pointed at the bloody shirt. "Looks like he was stabbed twice. The shirt is ripped here as well," he said, indicating a blood-soaked area near the victim's shoulder.

"If my anatomy is correct, the second blow is right through the heart," Hank said. "That's the one that killed him." He leaned in, squinted, then looked at King. "There's something in his mouth. I'd say it's a rosebud."

King looked closer. "That connects it to Adam Thorburn, no doubt."

"Morning, Hank, King."

Hank glanced toward the sound of the voice. It was Nancy Pietek. The medical examiner stepped gingerly over the broom and approached the body.

"Morning, Nancy," Hank said, moving back to give the ME some room to crouch down and do a preliminary inspection.

Nancy glanced at the victim as she pulled on a pair of surgical gloves. She rolled the body slightly, lifted the victim's shirt and peered at his back. She tested the joints, felt the skin, then looked at Hank and announced, "Time of death approximately twelve hours ago."

Hank glanced at his watch. "About nine o'clock last night."

"How accurate is that?" King asked.

Nancy looked at King. "Pretty close. Perhaps a half hour either way."

King turned to Hank. "The timestamp on the email was nine fifty-four, so assuming Nancy is accurate on the time of death, it looks like the message was sent after the victim died."

"Which means the killer sent the email," Hank said.

Nancy leaned over the body. She worked the victim's mouth open, reached in with two fingers, and removed a rosebud. She held it up for the detectives to see. "It appears to be the same as the last one."

Hank squinted at the rose. "Looks the same to me."

Nancy tucked it into an evidence bag. "I'll get it checked out to be sure."

Hank stood and glanced down the hallway toward the exit. There was a door on one wall of the corridor. He moved down the hall, stepped over the glass, and opened the door. His eyes roved around a small supply room. Tools hung neatly on the walls, more on a workbench. A box of fluorescent bulbs leaned in a corner, a coil of electrical wire on the floor, a power saw resting on a sawhorse.

His attention was caught by an empty spot on the wall where a screwdriver should be hanging along with the rest of the set. It had to be the murder weapon.

He glanced around the room again, then moved back into the corridor and shut the door. King beckoned toward him from the end of the hallway.

Hank went toward King and followed him past the body. King pointed at the floor. Hank crouched down and frowned at the spots of red, spaced at even intervals, leading from the body, through the door, and into the main area of the school. Hank followed the patches. They faded away after a few feet.

Hank stood and looked at King. "The killer tracked

through the blood, then went down this hallway."

"Probably to send the email," King said.

Jameson approached them. "We got some photos of that. It looks like we have clear footprints near the body, less clear as we move this way. Probably about a size eleven shoe."

"Size eleven," Hank said, his brow wrinkled. "If I recall correctly, the report on the search of the Thorburn house noted Adam Thorburn's shoes are a size eleven."

King dug the email from his pocket and handed it to Jameson. "See if you can find out what computer this was sent from." He pointed at the return email address. "Likely from the main office."

Jameson took the email and browsed it. "Shouldn't be a problem," he said. "We'll find the computer and check for prints."

Hank looked at King. "Are we done here? Can you think of anything else?"

King shrugged. "I think we have it covered."

"Then let's get out of here and catch this guy," Hank said. "Why don't you see if you can find any of the staff who knew our victim? They might be able to shed some light on this."

"Will do, Hank."

"I need to talk to the Lincolns, then I have to find out if Mr. Ronson has any next of kin and make a visit."

Hank moved back into the corridor, gazed down at the body, and sighed. Despite the pale white face, the victim still had a gentle look about him. Raymond Ronson didn't seem like the kind of guy who would harm anyone, and it angered Hank.

The senseless death of innocent victims always did that to him. And it wasn't just the death of the victim. It affected the person's family, friends, and everyone around him.

More than one person's life had been changed forever because of this violent act. Hank gazed at the body and doubled his vow to track down Adam Thorburn and bring him to justice any way he could.

CHAPTER 20

Wednesday, 9:52 a.m.

JAKE LEANED against the fender of the Firebird, his arms crossed, watching the proceedings outside the school. He glanced over toward Annie. She was chatting with one of the uniformed officers whose task it was to keep the crowd from getting too close.

Jake wanted to find out if Hank had discovered anything during his study of the crime scene that would help in the search for Adam Thorburn. He wasn't all that particular about who eventually found the killer; whether it was them or Hank, he didn't care, he only wanted Thorburn tracked down like the dog he was.

He looked toward the service door as Hank stepped out,

removed his shoe coverings and rolled them up, stuffing them into a side pocket of his jacket. The cop glanced toward Jake, raised a finger, and spoke to the officer at the door.

An investigator carried a bag of something from the building and put it into the forensic van. They would be here awhile yet, making sure nothing was missed. No matter how small or how large, everything would be thoroughly scrutinized and documented.

The ambulance had pulled away some time ago, replaced by the coroner's van. A pair of guys stood outside the van, talking and waiting. When the body was ready for them, they would bypass the hospital and carry their load directly to the city morgue.

The ME had driven away a few minutes earlier. Nancy's task had only begun, her thorough study of the body yet to take place before the victim could be allowed to rest in peace.

Hank finished his chat and he came toward Jake, shaking his head. "It looks like the work of Thorburn," the cop said.

Annie must've been keeping an eye out for Hank. She appeared beside Jake and spoke to the cop. "Was that a rose in his mouth?"

Hank nodded grimly. "It looks to be the same species as the last one. The lab'll soon tell us if it is."

"If so, then there's no way this is a copycat," Annie said.

Hank agreed. "A few people knew about the rose in the last victim's mouth, but no one outside the department knows exactly what species it is."

"What about the email?" Jake asked. "Any idea if it was the killer or the victim who sent it?"

"According to the time of death Nancy gave, it had to be the killer. Rod Jameson's trying to track down the computer it was sent from." Hank turned his head away, gazing toward the road. A disgusted look appeared on his face and he motioned with a jerk of his head. "It's Lisa Krunk," he said.

Jake followed Hank's gaze. The Channel 7 Action News van drove across the parking lot and stopped outside the taped-off perimeter. The doors swung open. Lisa Krunk stepped from the passenger side, her cameraman, Don, from the other. Don slid open the side door, removed a camera, and dropped it onto his shoulder. He hurried to catch up with Lisa as she strode toward the tape and stopped.

"Detective Corning," Lisa called, waving with one hand, a microphone held securely in the other.

Hank sighed. "I guess I should talk to Lisa." He turned to Jake. "Don't go anywhere. I'll need to get your statements later."

"We're right with you," Jake said, glancing at Annie. They followed Hank over to where the reporter stood, her wide mouth cracked into a tight-lipped smile.

They'd had more than their share of run-ins with the pushy reporter before. Jake knew Lisa considered herself a world-class journalist, yet to come into her own. Jake knew otherwise. Her sensational stories often had a scandalous twist to them as she played fast and loose with the truth. He expected this time would be no different.

But even with all her shortcomings, Jake had to admit, the nosy reporter occasionally came up with something useful to an investigation—for a price, of course. Lisa did little that didn't benefit her in some way.

"Good morning, Detective Corning," Lisa said, leaning into the tape, her long nose raking the mike as she spoke.

Hank nodded politely. "Good morning."

Lisa flashed a fake smile toward the Lincolns. Annie smiled back, her smile every bit as sincere as Lisa's.

Don stood slightly back and off to one side, the red light on his camera already glowing. He would capture everything, and later, Lisa would sculpt it into something that suited her own aspirations. Her editing skills were designed to shock, and however immoral, she was good at what she did.

"Detective Corning," Lisa began, her dark, painted eyes growing serious. "What can you tell the viewers about what happened here today?"

Hank took a deep breath and let it out slowly, giving himself time to form an answer. "A man was killed inside the school last night, and his body was discovered this morning."

Lisa's red lips flapped as she spoke. "Can you tell me who the victim was?"

Hank frowned. "You know better than that, Lisa. We can't release that information until we've notified the next of kin."

Lisa continued, unashamed. "Was he a teacher at this school?"

"I'm afraid I can't give you much right now. It was a homicide, and investigators are still going over the scene."

Lisa persisted. "Is this related to the murder on Monday evening that took place at North Richmond High?"

"It's too early in the investigation to tell yet."

"As you know," Lisa continued, "I've been continually broadcasting the face of Adam Thorburn, who's wanted in that murder. And I'll continue to do so until he's found."

"And we appreciate that, Lisa," Hank said, avoiding her subtle hint. "But it's too soon to draw any kind of connection between the two homicides."

Jake saw Lisa's mind at work as she wracked her brain to come up with another question. Then her eyes narrowed and she turned to Jake. "If this case isn't related, then why is Lincoln Investigations here? I happen to know they're looking into the murder of Nina White."

Jake looked at Annie, who was shaking her head in disgust. She moved away, wandering toward the school. Jake grinned to himself. His wife didn't have a lot of patience with Lisa Krunk. And truthfully, Jake didn't either, but the camera was running, so he would be as polite as possible.

Hank turned to Lisa. "They're here because they're running a parallel investigation, and I can't speak for them."

Lisa swung the microphone toward Jake, the same question in her eyes.

"I'm sorry," Jake said. "We have to respect the rights of our client and keep the reason for our involvement confidential."

Lisa shook her head in frustration and turned back to Hank. "Is there anything else you can tell me?"

"A complete statement will be forthcoming to all members of the press in due time," Hank said. "I have nothing else I can give you right now."

Lisa caught Don's eye and motioned toward the school. Don moved the camera away, walking around the perimeter. He would be getting whatever shots might help turn what little they knew into a short news story.

Lisa turned off the mike and flashed a polite smile. "Thank you, Detective," she said and turned to Jake. "Thank you, Jake."

Jake and Hank turned away and went to join Annie. She gave a weak smile as they approached. "I just didn't have any patience for that woman today."

"That's understandable," Hank said, shrugging. "I wouldn't talk to her either if I didn't need to." He paused, glancing toward the school. "Right now I have to find the victim's next of kin and make a visit." He looked at his watch. "Can I meet you guys at the precinct in about an hour to get your statements?"

Annie nodded. "We have a few things to take care of this afternoon, but we can work that in first."

"See you then," Hank said. He turned, walked toward his vehicle, and disappeared inside.

Jake turned to Annie. "It looks like we're going to have a busy day."

"That's fine by me," Annie said. "As long as it leads us closer to Adam Thorburn."

CHAPTER 21

Wednesday, 10:31 a.m.

HANK ALREADY had Raymond Ronson's address from his driver's license, but he wanted a little more information on the man before proceeding with the uncomfortable task he now faced. He gave Callaway a call and waited on the line while the cop looked up the information on Raymond Ronson.

He wondered if he would ever get used to being a homicide detective. Many years ago, he'd been taught never to get emotionally invested with the victims, just do his job and get on with it. But he'd never been able to do that. He took the murder of innocent victims personally, and he knew if he stopped caring, he wouldn't be able to do his job effectively.

His heart sank when he heard the news from Callaway. Raymond Ronson had a wife. Her name was Eunice and she was sixty-seven years old. Probably married to the same man all of her life, and now the news was going to tear her apart.

"She lives at 827 Flamingo Pond Road," Callaway continued. "No kids. No driver's license registered in her name. I checked missing persons reports, and even though her husband never come home last night, she didn't report it yet."

"Thanks, Callaway," Hank said. He hung up the phone, took a deep breath, and started the car, pulling from the lot. He knew exactly where he was headed, and knew the area well.

Fifteen minutes later, Hank turned onto an old winding road and descended into a valley. Flamingo Pond Road was in a picturesque part of the city, like a small, peaceful village secluded from the madness surrounding it. Flamingo Pond lay quietly at the heart of the community, with small houses on large lots in all directions. The waters of the pond sparkled in the midmorning sunlight, large, shady trees dotting the parklike area.

Number 827 was similar to the houses surrounding it. Set on a half acre of land, the century-old dwelling backed onto Flamingo Pond. Mature trees lined the driveway, with manicured dark green grass on all sides of the well-maintained house. Flowers bloomed in abundance along the front of the building, more in a handful of flowerbeds scattered throughout the property.

Hank pulled into the long driveway and stopped in front

of the garage, painted white with dark gray trim to match the rest of the house. Raymond had taken loving care of the entire property, and Hank wondered what would happen to the maintenance of this beautiful little place now.

He grabbed his briefcase from the passenger seat, climbed wearily from the vehicle, and walked up the flagstone walkway to the large front verandah. He hesitated a moment, his hand on the brass knocker, and then clanked it three times and waited.

In a few moments, the door swung inward and a little woman stood in the doorway. Not more than five foot two, with beautiful gray hair, a slightly rounded face, and a pleasantly plump build, she was the picture of everyone's grandmother.

"May I help you?" she asked. Hank saw apprehension on her face as she waited for him to speak.

"Eunice Ronson?" Hank asked.

"Yes, I'm Eunice Ronson."

Hank cleared his throat. "I'm Detective Hank Corning."

The woman gasped and her hand shot to her mouth, her brown eyes widening.

"May I come in a moment?" Hank asked.

Eunice remained frozen a moment and then slowly lowered her hand, her eyes still wide. She spoke in a hoarse whisper. "Is this about Raymond? My husband?"

"I'm afraid so, ma'am." Hank took a breath. "May I come in?"

Eunice stood back and Hank stepped inside. She closed the door and motioned toward the front room.

Hank walked into the room and sat uneasily on the edge of the couch, putting his briefcase on the floor beside him.

Eunice sat in a matching chair and faced him, her back straight, her hands gripped tightly together in her lap. "He didn't come home last night," she said softly, her aging face now lined with worry and fear.

Hank took a deep breath. "Mrs. Ronson, I'm sorry to tell you, your husband was ... killed last night."

Eunice took a sharp breath and held it, her wide eyes drilling into Hank's. She breathed again, rapidly, then one word came out, spoken in disbelief. "Killed?"

Hank nodded. "I'm sorry, ma'am."

"How? What happened?"

This was going to be the hard part. Death of a loved one was always impossible to take, but an untimely death at the hands of another was almost unimaginable.

"I'm afraid he was murdered, Mrs. Ronson."

Eunice took another sharp breath and shook her head rapidly. "No. No. It can't be." She paused, frozen, her hand over her mouth, and then her shoulders slumped and she dropped her head.

Hank remained still, watching her grief, his own heart breaking.

Then she raised her head, lifted her chin, her eyes filled with anger. "Who did it? Who killed him?"

"We aren't sure yet, ma'am. Mr. Ronson's body was found this morning. We have a suspect, but the investigation has just begun." Hank explained where the body was found and how her husband was killed.

When he was finished, tears were rolling down her cheeks. She found a tissue in the pocket of her dress and dabbed at her eyes. "Raymond loved that school," she said quietly. "He worked there for many years and loved his job and the kids." She sighed, her whole body slumping.

Hand picked up his briefcase and put it on the couch beside him, flipping it open. He removed a photo of Adam Thorburn and held it up for Mrs. Ronson to see. "Do you recognize this man?"

She leaned in and shook her head. "Is that the man who killed my Raymond?"

"It's possible," Hank said. "His name is Adam Thorburn. Does that name sound familiar? Perhaps Raymond might've mentioned it?"

She shook her head again. "I don't recall hearing the name."

"Would you know of anyone else who might've wished your husband any harm?"

"Oh, no. Nobody would want to hurt Raymond. He was loved by everybody. We've been married for fifty-one years, Detective." Her fingers went to her wedding ring, twirling it while she spoke. "We were just babies when we got married, but I don't regret a day of it. My Raymond was the sweetest man I've ever known." Her eyes roved around the spotless room. "We've lived in this house since we got married."

"It's a beautiful house," Hank said. "Well taken care of." He paused and looked intently at Eunice. "Can you think of anything else that might help us?"

She blew her nose gently, then looked at Hank and shook her head. "Did this Adam not admit to it?"

"We're unable to locate him at the moment," Hank said.

She took a quivering breath and leaned back in her chair, closing her eyes. When she opened them, she whispered, "May I see my husband?"

"Soon," Hank said. "The medical examiner is taking good care of him, and I'll let you know as soon as you can see him."

"Thank you, Detective."

"Mrs. Ronson, do you have anyone who can stay with you for a while?"

She nodded and forced a weak smile. "I have a sister close by. She lost her husband a few years ago and lives alone." She glanced around the room, her eyes resting on a photo perched on the mantel of a fireplace. It was a faded photo of a happy couple on their wedding day. "Perhaps I'll stay with her awhile."

"Let me know if you do," Hank said. "We'll need to keep in touch with you." He handed her a business card, snapped his briefcase closed, and stood. "I'll see myself out. Please call me if you need anything at all."

She nodded. "I will."

Hank left the heartbroken woman alone in her empty house as he left quietly and made his way back to his vehicle. He got in and drove away, more determined than ever to find her husband's killer.

CHAPTER 22

THE LINCOLNS stopped at a deli for an early lunch before heading to the precinct to meet Hank. When they arrived, they parked behind the building and went inside. Hank wasn't at his desk, and they were informed Detective King hadn't been in all day.

Annie left Jake chatting with Officer Spiegle at the front desk and wandered back to talk to Callaway. The cop looked up from his monitor, rocked his chair back, and grinned at her when she approached his desk.

"Hi, Annie. What brings you here?"

"Oh, nothing much. Just the usual murder and mayhem."

Callaway gave a short laugh, his face quickly turning somber. "Yeah, it's sad when this happens. From what I understand, both victims were great people."

"That's the worst thing about it," Annie said, then asked, "Has Hank shown up yet?"

"He went to see Ronson's wife out by Flamingo Pond. He should be here soon."

Annie was unaware of Raymond Ronson's domestic situation. She wasn't surprised to hear of his wife, but it saddened her. She would make a point of visiting the woman soon. A friendly word always went a long way in a heartbreaking situation.

"I traced the email back to a computer in the main office of the school," Callaway said. "Lots of people had access to it, and according to forensics, there're a lot of fingerprints."

"Any from Adam Thorburn?" Annie asked.

Callaway shook his head. "Forensics lifted Adam's prints from his mother's house, so we have something to compare them to, but no match."

"Any word yet if they found his prints anywhere else? Like on doorknobs or on the murder weapon?"

"Forensics is still processing the scene, and we don't have anything back from that end of things. Shouldn't be much longer. I guess Hank'll be the first to know." He cocked his head toward the front door. "Speak of the devil."

Annie followed Callaway's gaze. Hank was stopped at the front desk, talking to Jake. They looked her way and Hank gave a quick wave.

"Thanks, Callaway. I'll talk to you later," Annie said. She

went to Hank's desk and sat in a guest chair. Jake and Hank came over and took seats.

"I left King at the scene," Hank said. "He's talking to some of the staff, but I don't expect much from them." He pulled his chair in and reached into his drawer for a pad of blank police reports. "Let's get to it, shall we? It's just for the record. You've done it before and I'm sure you'll do it again."

They spent the next few minutes filling out an official report outlining the details of how they came to visit the school that morning and the events surrounding their discovery of Raymond Ronson's body.

When Annie finished, she signed the report and handed it to Hank. "Tell me about Raymond Ronson's wife," she said, sitting back.

Hank sighed, tucked the paper into a folder, and leaned back. "Eunice Ronson. She seems like a sweet old woman. Madly in love with her husband and completely torn up about it. Understandable, of course."

"And she's alone now?"

"Says she has a sister close by."

Annie was relieved to hear the woman had family, but decided she would visit Eunice anyway.

Jake spoke up. "Hank, was there anything at the scene that might lead you to believe the killer was anyone other than Adam Thorburn?"

"I don't have much back yet, but from what I saw, it all points to Thorburn. There were footprints in the blood, tracked into the school. Probably on his way to the computer. Size eleven shoes. Same as Thorburn's."

"And the rose in the victim's mouth," Jake said. "That sets a pattern."

Hank nodded. "That's the most telling fact. It's like a signature. Serial killers often leave a message of some kind." He shook his head and frowned. "I hope that's not what we're dealing with here."

"It's starting to fit the pattern," Annie said.

"I hope you're wrong."

"So do I." Annie leaned forward. "Callaway said Adam's prints weren't on the computer the email was sent from."

"Probably wore gloves," Jake put in.

Annie looked at Jake. "If he did, he probably would have had to take them with him when he ran. I'm not sure that would be on his mind at the time, and it's doubtful he would've picked them up later."

"He might've pulled his sleeve over his hand," Hank said. "It wouldn't be the first time."

"It strikes me as unusual both murders took place at a school," Jake said. "And both were schools Adam attended."

"And he would've known of Raymond Ronson," Hank added. "Ronson has been the janitor there for the last thirty years."

"But what's the significance of the schools?"

"We know he had a hard time at school," Hank said. "He was bullied and misunderstood. And he dropped out after two years of high school."

"If he was bullied, why not go after the bullies?" Annie asked. "Why the guidance counselor and the janitor?"

"I don't know," Hank said, shaking his head. "After all

these years, I still don't understand a killer's mind. I only know enough to expect the unexpected."

"Wherever he is," Jake said, "he came out of hiding long enough to kill and then hid again."

"And that's why I would love to be able to forecast his next move, but he's unpredictable. We have officers watching both schools round the clock in case he shows again. And cops are on the lookout city wide."

"Don't forget he has a high IQ, so he's intelligent," Jake said. "He'll have a good idea where you're watching for him."

"True, but serial killers are often impulsive and in need of instant gratification. That can make them careless."

Annie's cell phone rang and she looked at the caller ID. "It's Teddy White," she said, looking at Hank. "Do we have anything new I can tell him?"

Hank shrugged.

Jake shook his head.

Annie took a breath and answered the phone.

"Mrs. Lincoln," the caller's voice came from the phone. "It's Teddy White. Have you found Adam Thorburn yet?"

Annie thought quickly. "We've been following a few leads," she said. "Unfortunately, we haven't tracked him down yet, but we're giving it our full attention."

There was a sigh on the other end of the line, then, "The police have nothing for me either."

"I'll be sure to let you know if we have anything positive to report," Annie said.

"Thank you. I'll be waiting."

Annie hung up and made a wry face. "I guess if he's

paying us to investigate, he deserves to know what we're up to, but it's hard to continually tell him we have nothing for him."

Hank chuckled. "Better you than me."

Jake spoke up. "Hank, I have plans to visit Dr. Zalora a little later. He said he could squeeze a few minutes off his lunch break. Anything I should know?"

"You won't get much more than an expression of concern from him. He's pretty tight-lipped. Doctor-patient confidentially and all that."

"I'll give him a shot anyway," Jake said. "You never know. I'm willing to try anything even remotely helpful if it leads to finding Thorburn."

"I'm anxious to see the forensics report," Hank said. "But I assume if they found anything earth-shattering they would've let me know." He opened a folder on his desk and glanced at a sheet of paper. "I was able to get a list of Adam's classmates from the school. It might be a long shot, but I'm hoping one of them might have an idea where Adam's hiding out." He looked at his watch. "As soon as King gets here I want to get right on it. I don't have time to sit around."

"And we have things to do as well," Annie said, looking at Jake.

Jake stood. "We'll let you know if we find any interesting tidbits, Hank."

Hank gave a quick wave. "See you later, guys."

Annie stood and followed Jake from the precinct and out to the Firebird. They got in and she turned to Jake. "If Adam

Thorburn keeps to his schedule, he's going to kill someone again this evening."

"Then we need to get on his tail," Jake said, starting the vehicle. "If he knows we're coming, he might be afraid to make a move."

"I hope you're right," Annie said.

CHAPTER 23

Wednesday, 12:16 p.m.

ADAM THORBURN loved the swamp and the solitude it brought, but he missed the house he grew up in. He longed for his regular routine and peace of mind. But mostly, he missed his one true source of quiet and tranquility—the roses that grew along the back of the house—his roses, still surviving without his loving care.

He'd had a frightening experience the evening before. He had returned home, being careful no one saw him, and crept into the house through the basement window. There he'd raided the fridge, then grabbed a blanket and some clean clothes, leaving the ones he'd been wearing in the laundry basket. His mother would be sure to see them and realize he'd been there. Knowing he was alive would give her a small measure of peace.

On his way from the house, he had dug up one of his prize rosebushes to bring to his new home. He was careful to take enough soil to protect the roots, nestling it carefully in a plastic bag to protect it on the journey. He wanted to plant it near his hut, and even if the rest of them perished, he would faithfully nourish this one in the rich soil of the swamp.

Growing roses was perhaps the thing he enjoyed most in this world. They needed proper nutrition, and he nurtured them until they bloomed, careful to give them the perfect amount of water and nourishment. They responded to his painstaking attention by growing strong and healthy, and they never expected more from him than he was able to give. Those roses were what he missed most about home.

He remembered taking the rosebush back to the swamp and carefully planting it. He had taken his medication as usual, and then wandered out to explore the surrounding area.

Perhaps an hour or two later, he found himself outside the steel mill, away from his new home, with no idea how he'd gotten there. The last he knew, the sun had told him there were still a couple hours of daylight left, but suddenly it was dark.

He had blacked out and it frightened him. He could've been seen. Perhaps he was. There was no indication where he had been or what might've taken place during his lost period of time.

After that, he made his way carefully back to the swamp

and huddled in the corner while a panic attack overtook his senses. When his anxiety subsided, he lay down for the night, waking often from horrifying nightmares with only the sounds of his beloved swamp to calm his tortured mind.

And now, as he huddled in the corner of his shack, he feared it could happen again, and this time he might get caught. Part of him wished to be finally found out and given the punishment he knew he truly deserved, but the fear of the further torment that would bring overcame his feeble desire to surrender.

He reached into his pocket and pulled out a wrinkled business card. The name on the card was Lincoln Investigations. He'd found it on the kitchen table and assumed they'd come to talk to his mother, looking for him. He knew the police were after him, and as if that wasn't bad enough, now a private firm was on his trail as well.

He wondered who had hired them. Was it his mother, trying to help him in some way? That didn't seem likely. She had barely enough money to pay for his medication and put food on the table, and anyway, there wasn't much anyone could do for him now.

Perhaps they were working with the police. That was a frightening thought. Or maybe they'd been hired by the family of the woman he'd killed. In which case, they probably wouldn't stop coming for him until they tracked him down. The private investigators he knew from movies and TV usually operated outside the law, doing whatever it took to find their prey.

The thought filled him with terror and he felt another

panic attack overtaking him. He shook his head and went outside the hut. He stepped down the slope, halfway to the swampy waters, and crouched down beside the rosebush. He caressed the petals, careful not to injure them, and a peace came over him once again, soothing his soul and easing his mind.

He wondered what it was about the roses that calmed him. Perhaps because the perfect beauty of the red flowers were such a sharp contrast to the pathetic ugliness inside of him. They reminded him of how he longed to be—healthy and loved. They gave him a dream for a better day, even when he knew he was beyond all hope, beyond any chance of redemption.

Adam sat on the grass beside the bush and pulled up his knees. He gazed into the tepid waters of the swamp, wondering about the person he had killed. His mother had told him it was a woman and that's all he knew. Even though he didn't know her name or anything about her, he mourned for her.

Did she have family? She most probably did and they would he heartbroken. He mourned for them as well, wishing he could make it better, take back what he'd done and start fresh. But that was impossible.

The only thing he could do was make sure it never happened again. That meant he would either have to surrender, a dreadful thought, or end his own life. He wasn't sure if he had the strength to do that, but it was the best solution. It wasn't a way out for him; it was for the protection of others.

Whether he surrendered to the police, or gave his useless life to the swamp, his mother would be heartbroken. She'd told him to run for his own protection. He wondered if that was a selfish move on her part and if he was being selfish as well. Was it wrong for him to cling to his own worthless life when there was a better way?

He stood and looked toward the bright blue sky and howled in anguish. He clenched his fists, praying to a God he didn't know. He'd made up his mind—this was for the best, and he was determined to go through with it no matter what. He only hoped God would understand and forgive him.

He summoned all his inner strength and continued down the slope, stepping into the regenerating water. His feet sank into the oozing mud and soaked his ankles. He gritted his teeth and took another step, the water now deeper. A few more steps and the warm water lapped at his chest. He lifted his head, howled with emotional pain, took a deep breath, and dove into the black water.

He sank to the muddy bottom, dying vegetation and slime caressing his body. Soon he would have to breathe and that's when he would die. He thought of home, his mother, the bullies at school, and his father. He thought of the life he'd taken and he screamed inside. Finally, he took a breath, felt the warm water enter his lungs, and knew it would soon be over.

Then as if he were controlled by some outside force, his feet pushed at the muddy bottom, propelling him upwards into the warm air. He took a breath, choked, tried to breathe again, and coughed up swampy water. He struggled to reach the bank, gasping for air. Finally, he pulled himself up and lay panting on the dark green grass at the edge of the swamp.

He didn't even have the strength or willpower to kill himself, and he cursed his own cowardliness as he huddled in a fetal position and cried.

CHAPTER 24

Wednesday, 12:54 p.m.

JAKE PULLED his Firebird into the Central Plaza parking lot and slipped into a slot near the door leading to offices on the second floor.

He swung from the vehicle and entered the small lobby, checking the directory. The office of Dr. Zalora was in Suite 201. He climbed the stairs two at a time, stopped in front of 201, and pushed the door open.

The receptionist looked up as he entered, a well-practiced smile on her otherwise plain face. "May I help you?"

Jake handed her his business card. "I have an appointment with Dr. Zalora."

She consulted a pad on her desk, picked up the intercom,

and spoke into the receiver. She hung up and motioned toward a row of comfortable chairs. "Have a seat. Dr. Zalora will be with you shortly."

Jake sat and looked around the small waiting room. The usual supply of magazines was stacked on a coffee table, modern art prints on the white walls, cheap carpeting under his feet. He grabbed a magazine, flipped through it, and tossed it back down.

The receptionist tapped keys on a keyboard as classical music played in the background. Then a door behind her popped open and a man stood in the doorway, his eyes on Jake. "Mr. Lincoln?" the man asked.

Jake nodded and stood, extending his hand as he approached.

"I'm Dr. Zalora," the man said, shaking Jake's hand. He stepped aside and motioned toward the office. "Come in, please."

Jake stepped into the large office and glanced around. Except for the massive mahogany desk against one wall, it looked more like a sitting room than an office. Designed to put patients at ease, the room was filled with comfortable chairs, couches, and antique-style end tables. Fine art prints decorated the light blue walls. The noon sun eased between the wooden slats of a large window on the outside wall, casting a warm glow across the hardwood floor.

Dr. Zalora waved toward a padded guest chair on the near side of the desk. Jake sat as the doctor moved behind his desk, sat down, and leaned back comfortably, his elbows on the armrests, his fingers steepled under his chin.

The doctor was of average height, possibly in his early forties. A well-tailored suit covered his thin build, a white shirt and red tie completing the look. His dark hair had a wide strip of blond across the front, hanging down to his eyebrows. Jake thought it looked rather ridiculous in comparison to his otherwise professional look.

"I only have a few minutes," Dr. Zalora said. "I understand you're interested in Adam Thorburn?"

Jake dug out another business card, handed it to the doctor, and nodded. "I'm sure you're aware of the murders that have taken place in the past two days and the suspicions of Adam's involvement."

"I am," the doctor said. "I discussed Adam's condition briefly with a detective yesterday. I'm not sure how I can help you other than what I've already given the police. You must understand, other than my general diagnosis, patient confidentiality precludes me from discussing certain areas."

"I understand," Jake said. "My concern is in finding Adam Thorburn and I'm only interested in his condition as far as it relates to his motives and possible future actions."

"Adam is a rather unusual case," the doctor said, leaning forward. The blond streak fell across one eye and he brushed it back with a hand. "Are you aware he's schizophrenic?"

Jake nodded.

The doctor narrowed his eyes in thought. "Schizophrenics rarely display aggressive or violent behavior, in fact, no more than the average person. There are exceptions, of course, but generally any display of aberrant behavior is often due to the subject's background and other environmental factors."

"And in Adam's case?"

The doctor thought a moment longer. "In Adam's case, in addition to schizophrenia and all that involves, he occasionally displays psychopathic and sociopathic tendencies."

"Meaning?"

"Meaning, on occasion, he shows abnormal or violent social behavior combined with a lack of conscience."

"And that's what led him to murder?" Jake asked.

"Partially, yes, although extremes like that wouldn't necessarily be evident unless he already had a tendency in that direction."

"In other words," Jake said, "he's already crazy, and all those big words make him crazier?"

The doctor chuckled. "I wouldn't put it exactly like that, but in layman's terms, it's a fair interpretation."

"So how can all this help me find him?" Jake said.

"I'm afraid it might not be all that helpful. Adam is highly intelligent but unpredictable." The doctor sighed. "What makes this case disturbing is that Adam, when behaving normally, is rather a likable young man. He seems to be in a struggle with himself, and I believe that's why he doesn't remember his actions on occasion. He has periods with either no memory, or a hazy recollection of certain events. His subconscious is at work, suppressing his memory of incidents abhorrent to his normal personality."

"He's a complex person," Jake said.

"A very complex personality, indeed."

"What about medications?" Jake asked. "Other than what

he now takes, is there nothing different he can try?"

The doctor shook his head, his shock of blond drooping. He brushed it back again. "Adam hasn't responded favorably to any of the usual medications." He raised his hands as if in surrender. "We've tried everything as well as a variety of combinations. His situation has worsened since his father died, and there seem to be no answers."

"According to Detective Corning, there're some new, more aggressive medications," Jake said.

"Yes, there are, but they're costly, and as I'm sure you're aware, the Thorburns are not in the best financial position. Additionally, there's no guarantee he would respond favorably to any of them."

Jake looked at the doctor, struggling to find an answer in all he heard. He was getting a lot of information but didn't see how any of it could help him find Adam Thorburn.

"I understand Adam likes solitude," Jake said. "During your sessions with him, did he give you any indication of places he liked to go to be alone?"

"He wanders off occasionally," the doctor said. "But for the most part, he prefers to stay home, generally in the isolation and privacy of his bedroom. His withdrawal has been more pronounced recently—again, since his father died—and I believe it also stems from his childhood history of being bullied for being different."

"What significance do roses have to him?"

"He loves growing roses. It brings him peace. To him, it's the only source of beauty in an otherwise ugly world."

"Dr. Zalora, did Adam ever mention any love interest to

you?" Jake asked. "Anyone specifically?"

The doctor shook his head. "He often expressed his desire to find someone, but he also realized that in his condition it was impossible. It's a source of sadness for him."

"His first murder was Nina White," Jake said. "The counselor at North Richmond High. The police have a theory Adam had a secret crush on her and killed her because he couldn't have her." Jake paused. "Do you think that's a possibility?"

"I can't say, either personally or professionally, but it's a possibility. I've been unable to find out what goes on in Adam's mind when he's in an aggressive mood."

"The second victim was a janitor at Millfield Elementary School, the primary school Adam attended," Jake said. "Do you see any significance in that?"

The doctor pursed his lips a moment. "Adam hated school, and he might be taking his hatred out on anyone connected with school. They might not have been targeted personally, just by association." Dr. Zalora looked at his Rolex.

Jake leaned forward. "Anything else you can add that might help find Adam?"

"I think we've just about covered it." Dr. Zalora stood. "I have to rush. I have other appointments." He came out from behind the desk and held out his hand. "Please let me know if you find Adam."

Jake stood and shook hands with the doctor. "Thank you for your time. I'll be sure to let you know if I have anything positive to report."

Dr. Zalora smiled politely as Jake turned and left the office. The doctor had given him a lot to think about. It helped him understand more about what they faced, but he wasn't sure how any of it would lead to finding Adam Thorburn before he killed another innocent person.

CHAPTER 25

Wednesday, 1:21 p.m.

ANNIE HAD ARRANGED to interview the Thorburns' neighbor, Mabel Shorn, at 1:30 in the afternoon. Virginia Thorburn's closest friend promised she would be available at that time, no problem, she was home most of the day anyway.

Number 114 Mill Street wasn't much different from the dwellings surrounding it—a small clapboard house, cheaply built and run-down. Annie pulled her Escort into the gravel driveway, stopping in front of a detached single-car garage, built many years ago to match the design of the house. The wooden garage door sagged and likely hadn't been opened for years.

She picked her handbag up off the passenger seat and

stepped out, moving around the rear of the car to the side door. The inner door was open, and the aluminum screen door rattled as she tapped on it. A woman got up from the kitchen table, leaving her cigarette in the ashtray, and came to the door.

Mabel Shorn was scrawny, all skin and bones, her track pants barely held up by her small, bony hips. Smoke trailed from her thin mouth as she pushed the door open. She brushed back a strand of long dyed-red hair and motioned with her head for Annie to come in.

Annie stepped inside. The woman had already moved back to her spot at the table, reaching for her smoke. She took a drag as Annie pulled back a hard wooden chair and sat down, setting her handbag on a free spot on the crowded table.

She held out her hand. "I'm Annie Lincoln."

The woman gave Annie's hand a weak shake and blew smoke in the air. "Mabel," she said, her voice hoarse from too many cigarettes. "Want coffee?"

"No, thanks."

"Want a beer?"

Annie shook her head and Mabel shrugged. She picked up her coffee mug, downed the last swallow, and set it down with a clunk, pushing it back into the rest of the mess on the table.

"Police were already here yesterday," Mabel said. "Asked me a bunch of questions about Adam. Couldn't tell them much." She shrugged. "Not much to tell."

"I realize that," Annie said. "But thanks for seeing me anyway."

"Might as well. I'm not busy." Mabel turned her head and gave a loud yawn, sucking her cheeks deeper into her already gaunt face. She dug around on the table, flipped a magazine aside, and found a business card. "Detective Hank Corning was here." She waved the card. "Said I should call him if I think of anything."

"I know Detective Corning," Annie said. "He's a good cop."

"Seems like it," Mabel said. She gave a lopsided grin and tossed the card on the table. "Nice looking, too."

Annie smiled, paused, and cleared her throat. "As I told you on the phone, we were hired to find Adam Thorburn."

"It's a bit of a shame, that is," Mabel said. "Doesn't seem like the type to go off and do something like that."

"You're aware Adam is schizophrenic?" Annie asked.

"Sure, I know he's nutty from time to time, but never have I seen him hurt nobody." She shrugged and took a drag of her cigarette, blowing the smoke in a thin line over Annie's head. "Course, I seen him fighting with some neighborhood punks once or twice. They started it, though. Can't leave the kid alone, it seems."

"How long have you known Adam?" Annie asked.

"Since he was a little kid. Going on ten years now I guess. That's how long Ed and me been here." She jerked a thumb. "Ed works at the steel mill."

"Considering the amount of time you've known Adam, do you have any idea where he might be?"

Mabel turned her eyes upward, picking at a tooth with an extra-long, painted fingernail before speaking. "I know he takes off once in a while. By himself. Virginia tells me sometimes he's gone all day and comes home late. Not sure where he goes, though."

"Have you seen him in the last two days?"

Mabel butted her smoke in an overflowing ashtray. "Nope. Virginia tells me he's gone off. She don't know where either."

Annie nodded thoughtfully and took a deep breath. "If you recall the night Adam took the car out, Monday evening, Virginia was here with you. Did you happen to hear Adam leave or come back?"

Mabel gave a hollow laugh. "Didn't hear nothing. Ed was working overtime, some kind of emergency at the mill, so me and Virginia had a few beers." She grinned. "I wasn't feeling much pain that night." Her face sobered. "Virginia told me the next day what happened. She was kicking herself something awful for leaving Adam alone. She said he felt down and now she feels guilty."

"He's an adult," Annie said. "She can't be responsible for everything Adam does."

"Sure enough," Mabel said, yawning again. She sat forward. "She ain't like me, you know. She's got a bit of class. More refined I guess they say. Sure we get drop-dead drunk once in a while, but she's more of a lady if you know what I mean. No pretenses either. She is what she is and I am what I am." She sat back and chuckled. "But we get along okay."

Annie smiled politely. "It's always nice to have a good friend."

"We're closer since her husband died. Guess she has more

time on her hands now and the booze helps her cope." She lit another cigarette and took a couple of long drags. "Her husband worked at the mill too, you know. Got killed there. Some kind of an accident with the machinery. Killed him instantly." She shook her head. "I tell Ed he better be careful. Could happen to him."

"How long ago was that?" Annie asked.

Mabel frowned and bit her lip thoughtfully. "Guess it's going on a year now or thereabouts."

"Have you noticed any changes in Adam since that time?"

"Can't say as I did, but I wouldn't notice. I don't see him a lot, you know. Like I said, I hang out with Virginia but the kid don't come around much."

"Do you think your husband, Ed, might know where we can find Adam?"

"Nah. Him and Adam don't talk. Ed works hard, you know. Comes home from work and wants to put his feet up, relax, have a beer." She shrugged. "He deserves it. Works his butt off all day for crappy pay."

Annie cleared her throat. "Do you know if Adam ever had a girlfriend?"

Mabel threw her head back and laughed, quickly covering her mouth. "I guess it's not funny. Poor kid. I don't think any girl would go near him. Not for long anyway. Not with his problems." She shook her head. "Nope. Far as I know, he's never had a girlfriend."

Annie felt like she wasn't making much headway in finding out where Adam could be hiding. She'd run out of questions and hoped Jake did a little better. She opened her handbag and removed a business card, handing it to Mabel. "You can get ahold of me here any time."

Mabel took the card and set it on top of Hank's card.

"Please let me know if you see Adam. Or let the police know. It's important we find him right away."

Mabel nodded. "I'll call you if I see him. Like I said, Virginia's a good friend and I got nothing against the kid, but if he's going around killing, it sure ain't a good thing."

Annie stood and picked up her handbag. "Thanks for your time," she said.

The woman saw her to the door and pushed it open. "Sure hope this all works out, Annie. It was good to meet you."

Annie smiled, waved a hand, and stepped outside, making her way to the car. She sent Jake a text message to tell him she was on her way, then started the car and drove toward home.

CHAPTER 26

Wednesday, 1:45 p.m.

JAKE DROVE SLOWLY up and down the streets surrounding the Thorburn residence. According to Dr. Zalora, Adam Thorburn preferred to be at home whenever possible. It seemed likely Adam would never wander far from the only home he'd ever known. And though Dr. Zalora said Adam liked to be alone, there was little doubt he had to surface eventually.

With the entire city on the lookout for the fugitive, his only source of food and other necessities would be his mother's house.

Jake turned onto Steel Road and pulled over. On the left, houses similar to the rest of the neighborhood lined the street. To his right, a vast area housed the steel mill. Set on a score of acres, the mill employed hundreds of workers, many from the immediate area.

Vast smokestacks reached into the clouds, spewing out smoke, darkening the sky. Massive cranes dotted the skyline, moving rolls, coils, and raw materials to and fro. A faint smell, like rotten eggs—sulfur—permeated the air.

A flatbed truck exited the two-lane road leading into the mill. It rumbled past, carrying a load of colossal beams destined for a construction site somewhere in the city.

Jake reached into the backseat for a pair of binoculars and trained them on the sidewalk running down one side of the long street. A few pedestrians trod the concrete walkway. Some were workers, swinging a lunch box or paper sack, on their way to the afternoon shift at the mill. Others perhaps were out for a stroll, or heading to a neighbor's house to enjoy a cup of coffee and an afternoon of gossip.

He wound down his window, moved his glasses to the left, and gazed past a house to the adjoining property behind it, focusing on the rear of the Thorburn residence. Through the powerful lenses, he saw the rosebushes lining the back wall of the dwelling.

He scanned the neighborhood in all directions, training the glasses on anything that stirred, then turned back to the Thorburn house.

Leaning forward, he squinted through the lenses. Something moved. He sharpened the focus. The rear basement window swung open and Jake held his breath.

It could be Adam.

A figure squirmed from the window and stood, a grocery bag in one hand. Jake focused his binoculars on the face. It was Adam, no doubt.

He watched the figure stoop in front of a rosebush a moment, then stand, lope across the rear of the house, and disappear from view.

Jake tossed the binoculars onto the passenger seat, and the Firebird roared to life when he turned the key. The wheels spun on the soft shoulder, then caught on the asphalt as he swung the vehicle into a sharp U-turn.

He rounded the block, headed to Mill Street, and turned quietly onto the road. He continued at an idle, keeping a close eye out for the fugitive.

Adam was nowhere in sight.

He drove the entire block, scanning the sidewalks and properties until he reached the intersection, and then turned right and headed back to Steel Road.

His quarry had cut through a neighbor's property and was now approaching the sidewalk, the grocery bag swinging in one hand. Still two hundred feet away, Jake touched the gas and the car surged ahead.

Adam moved into the street, took a few steps, and stopped halfway across. He turned his head and froze a moment, staring at the car bearing down on him. Then the fugitive leaped into a run, crossed the street, and dashed toward the steel mill as Jake ground the Firebird to a stop on the shoulder and jumped out.

He charged ahead, his long legs cutting across the gravel and weeds. Adam approached one of the many ancillary buildings that dotted the property and disappeared behind it. Jake followed, spun around behind the structure, and stopped. Adam wasn't in sight. He could be hiding behind any of the buildings, maybe inside, or long gone.

Jake glanced around and listened for sounds of his quarry, straining to hear above the constant whine of machinery, rhythmic thumping, and screeches of metal on metal that came from the main building close by.

There were dozens of places to hide and scores of paths to freedom. Jake circled the nearby buildings, scouring the area, then continued toward the back of the property and approached a set of railroad tracks.

The engine of a powerful locomotive labored under a heavy load as it moved gradually forward, screeching in Jake's direction. He stepped across the tracks and looked in both directions as the train lumbered past.

A crash sounded a distance away when a crane dropped a load of scrap onto a stockpile, soon to be turned into molten metal.

Jake ran forward, his feet crunching on the gravel yard as he raced toward the rear of the property. The sounds of the mill lessened, becoming background noise, white noise, as he moved further away.

He stopped at a chain-link fence, ten feet high and barbed at the top, designed to keep the curious from wandering into danger. This was the absolute edge of the city. An empty field lay beyond, unused and overgrown, and a mile further on, a dark line of trees could be seen.

Then on the other side of the fence, fifty feet away, Adam

was plodding up the fence line, his head down as he moved toward Jake. He had made it around or through the fence and appeared to be circling back.

Jake glanced up. There was no way to climb over; the barbs at the top would stop him. He crouched down and waited. Adam still came, now twenty feet away.

Five feet away, the fugitive panted from the exertion of the chase, his breathing labored. So close, but out of reach.

Jake stood. "Adam Thorburn."

The fugitive stopped quick, his mouth open, staring wide-eyed through the links of the fence. He turned suddenly, ready to run, then stopped and spun back, his brow furrowed. He glared at Jake and spoke cautiously, his eyes narrowed. "What do you want?"

Jake studied the young man's face. He didn't look like a vicious killer, but Jake knew from past experience, looks can be deceiving.

"Why're you chasing me?" Adam asked with a puzzled frown.

"The police would like to talk to you."

Adam scowled. "I have no wish to talk to them."

"You can't run forever, Adam," Jake said.

"How do you know my name?"

"I've been looking for you. I want to help you."

Adam laughed. "I doubt that." His face sobered. "Nobody can help me. You must know that."

"Give yourself up and you'll see."

"Never." Adam tucked his hands into his pockets, the handle of the bag looped over his wrist. He raised his chin, his face darkening. "I know what would happen to me if I did."

Jake looked at the man who had killed in cold blood, not once, but twice, now defiant, desperate, and on the verge of running.

"I know you killed Nina White by accident," Jake said. "It wasn't your fault."

Panic gripped Adam's face. "Nina White? Mrs. White, the counselor at school?"

Jake nodded.

Adam seemed confused and took a step back. He opened his mouth to speak but no words came out. Then he took a deep breath and looked away. In a moment, he looked back, pain in his eyes. "I wouldn't hurt her. She was the only one who helped me. She believed in me when no one else did."

Jake tried one last plea. "That's why you need to surrender. We can get this all straightened out."

Adam's lips tightened and he shook his head adamantly.

Jake reached into his shirt pocket and removed a business card, tucking it through the fence. "Take my card. You can call me anytime."

Adam kept his eyes on Jake as he reached out carefully and snatched the card. He glanced at it and frowned. "You came to see my mother," he said, his eyes narrowed with suspicion.

"Yes, we did. She wants us to help you."

"Now I know you're lying. She would've left me a note and told me that if you only wanted to help." He took a step back and flipped the card through the air. It fell behind a tall weed. Adam turned, took a step, then glanced back. "Don't try to find me anymore. You never will. I'm heading west where you can never catch me."

As Adam jogged away, Jake ran along the fence, keeping pace with the fugitive. Before long, the fence stopped abruptly at a building, too high to scale, and too expansive to run around.

Jake watched helplessly as Adam disappeared into the distance. It was hopeless to give chase now; the man would soon be long gone.

CHAPTER 27

Wednesday, 2:55 p.m.

ANNIE'S CELL PHONE sounded, notifying her of a text message. It was Jake. He missed her and was on his way home. The message continued: "Have interesting news. Called Hank to drop by."

She pushed aside her notes and sat back in her swivel chair. It made sense to her, since Adam had killed a second person yesterday, that he was still in the area and wouldn't be leaving anytime soon. That gave them a better chance of catching him, but it also meant the killings might continue.

The motive for the murders stumped her. Adam knew Nina White, and he would most certainly have known who Raymond Ronson was. That was the only connection she

SILENT JUSTICE

could find, but that alone didn't seem like a powerful motive, and it was unlikely that discovering the reason behind it all would lead to Adam Thorburn.

The doorbell rang and she went to the front door and opened it.

Hank flashed a grin and stepped inside. "Jake not here yet?"

"He's coming home now," Annie said, leading the way to the living room.

"He said he had some news." Hank sat on the couch and set his briefcase beside him. "Between King and me, we've been able to get in touch with several of Adam Thorburn's classmates. We advised them of the possible danger and warned them to be on their guard."

"Both murders weren't just related to his schooldays, but actually took place at the schools," Annie noted. "And both were after hours."

"We have officers watching both buildings day and night. School security is on alert, with both schools on lockdown as much as possible during the day." Hank shrugged. "It's a necessary precaution, though it's doubtful Thorburn would hit the same place twice. He's too intelligent."

"True," Annie said. "But if it happens during one of his hazy periods, he might not be thinking clearly."

"That's why we're not taking any chances," Hank said. He turned his head toward the window as a car roared into the driveway. "Jake's here."

A moment later the front door opened, closed, and Jake stepped into the room. He nodded at Hank, pulled up an ottoman and sat, leaning forward, his arms resting on his legs.

"I ran into Adam Thorburn," he said.

Hank sat forward.

"I was watching the neighborhood," Jake said. "Watching his house and saw him leave through a basement window." His face twisted into a grimace. "I just missed him by a hair. Chased him across the yard of the steel mill, but somehow he got around the back fence." He grinned. "Had a little chat with him through the fence."

Hank's mouth hung open a moment, then he said, "You talked to him?"

Jake nodded and straightened his back. "He seemed genuinely surprised and upset when I mentioned Nina White. Said she was the only one who believed in him."

"He has a conscience when his sociopathic tendencies don't take over," Annie said.

"That's sort of what Dr. Zalora told me," Jake said. "He can be a normal kid most of the time, but on occasion he goes nuts."

"Did you get any indication where he might be hiding out?" Hank asked.

Jake shook his head. "No, but he said he was heading west where we'd never find him."

Hank sat back and rubbed his hands through his hair. "West? As far as we know, he has no family out west. His father's family lives east and north. We've been in contact with them and will continue to be, but if he's going west, he's on his own."

"Don't forget, he likes being on his own," Annie said.

"We'll get his photo out nationwide just the same," Hank said. "He might not be heading west. Why would he tell you that if it were true?"

"Maybe he wants us to think that," Annie said.

"Meaning?"

"Meaning he might not be leaving the city at all. I think we have to disregard what he said."

"I can't disregard it completely," Hank said. "But for the most part, all I can do is follow the evidence and see where it leads."

"What evidence?" Jake asked.

"From the crime scenes. I got a partial report from forensics. Adam's prints weren't found anywhere. The only prints on the screwdriver were those of Raymond Ronson. And Ronson's prints were also on the door handle along with yours, Jake." Hank looked at Annie. "And we found couple of yours on the wall near the light switch."

"And the computer the email was sent from?" Annie asked.

"All the prints were from office staff," Hank said, snapping open his briefcase. He removed a sheet of paper and browsed it. "According to the ME, the angle of penetration indicates Ronson was standing when he was stabbed. And CSI reports the killer tracked through the blood after the stabbing and made his way to the school computer."

"What about the rose?" Jake asked.

"Same species as the one found in Nina White's mouth. No surprise there."

"That's all fine," Annie said. "But we already know who

we're looking for. The question is, how do we find him?"

"We have officers all over the city looking for him. His face is in every newspaper and on every TV screen, and we're still canvassing and talking to anyone who knew him."

"What about outlying areas?" Annie asked. "Farms out of town, barns and other buildings?"

"All being covered," Hank said. "And King's still out there."

"What about the homeless community?" Jake asked. "Maybe he's staying with them. Hiding in plain sight."

Hank shook his head. "We've checked as much as possible, but a lot of them don't like to talk to cops. We've even contacted CIs. That's a dead end too. It's doubtful he ever associated with any of the criminal elements."

Annie leaned forward. "The only person he trusts is his mother."

"That might be," Hank said, "But she claims to have no idea where he is."

"She told us the same thing," Jake said. "But I'm not totally convinced."

"It looks like we might have to put an officer in the backyard of the Thorburn house," Hank said. "Watching the house from the front and patrolling the surrounding streets isn't sufficient."

"But that'll only keep him away," Annie said. "He's being rather careful."

"Possibly, but if he can't return home for food or supplies, it might force his hand," Hank said. He snapped his briefcase shut, picked it up, and stood. "I'd better get back at it. I have a few more people to see."

Annie sat back in her chair as Jake saw Hank to the door. When Jake returned and dropped onto the couch, she said, "I think we have to see if we can get something from Virginia Thorburn. I agree with you, she knows more than she's willing to say, and if so, she can't continue to cover for him if he keeps killing innocent people."

"Perhaps she knows something, but if not, somebody might," Jake said. "I'd like to figure out who he's going to target next. There has to be something we're missing. He's not killing at random. He knows the victims."

"That's the big puzzle. Since we don't know where he's hiding, we need to find out where he's heading. I wonder if you should stake out the neighborhood again in case he decides to return."

"It seems pretty unlikely now," Jake said. "Would he be that stupid?"

"Maybe," Annie said. "He does seem to be a little careless. Psychopaths don't have much fear and often leave clues purposely to bait the police. They have a desire to be known for their accomplishments and love to boast about them after they've been apprehended. Perhaps he subconsciously wants to be caught."

"He seemed pretty normal when I talked to him. He showed some remorse and displayed his conscience. I don't know if our chances of catching him are better when he's acting normal or when he's acting crazy."

"Either way, we have to do something soon," Annie said. "If there's one thing I know for certain, he's not finished killing. It's a question of who's next."

CHAPTER 28

Wednesday, 3:51 p.m.

ADAM THORBURN huddled against the wall of his shack, annoyed at himself for being seen, and afraid of any consequences his exposure might bring. He wouldn't be found in the swamp. They would never expect that, but it appeared they were still watching the neighborhood, and he wondered how long he would be safe.

It might be only a matter of time, and he shuddered at the thought of spending the rest of his life in prison. He would kill himself first. If they got too close, he would run as far as he could, but he would end it all before allowing himself to be captured.

He had no inclination to go out west. That was just

something he'd thought of off the top of his head. He wasn't even sure why he'd spoken to that nosy investigator. It didn't serve him any purpose and might make matters worse, and he felt jittery because of the encounter.

He opened the bag of supplies he'd brought back from the house. Along with a package of cold meats and some fresh fruit, his mother had left a further supply of medication in the fridge beside a freshly roasted chicken. She had expected him, and he was pleased at least one person in the world cared about his well-being.

Adam was famished, and he devoured half of the chicken, topping it off with a bottle of water. It made him feel better, at least for now. He carefully wrapped the remaining food in the bag, tied the top to keep out visiting insects, and set it on a shelf built into the wall of the hut. He would need a constant supply of food to keep him going, and he wasn't guaranteed where it would come from.

Though it was a warm day, he shivered in the heat, feeling anxious and uneasy, angry at the predicament he was in. He laid his head on a small pillow he'd brought from the house and covered up with the blanket. His mind was restless and his whole body trembled in fear.

He reached for his medications. He was taking them a little earlier than usual, but they always had a calming effect. He could use that right now. He worked a pill from each bottle, washed them down with water, and laid his head on the pillow. He was tired as well as afraid, and since he had little else to do, he decided to take a nap. Perhaps it would calm his nerves and bring him some peace of mind.

He was startled awake a few minutes later by the screech of an owl—a rare sound in the swamp. It reminded him of the mocking calls of the bullies at school, always teasing and torturing when all he wanted was to be left alone. The memories made him sad, and then angry. He blamed the bullies for the situation he was in now.

If his abusers had left him alone he wouldn't be in such a miserable mess. His mental condition was one he couldn't help; it wasn't his fault, and he raised his head and roared in frustration and anger, tears rolling down his face.

He wiped the tears on his sleeve, rolled to his feet, and went outside the hut. His rosebush still flourished, but somehow he didn't care about the roses anymore. At least, not right now.

Stooping down, he howled at the plant and leaned back as if expecting a response. He glared at the uncaring flower and then stood and straightened his back, his fists clenched, his eyes flared. He gazed at his surroundings a moment—at the decaying plants and the steaming bog—before striding away from the hut, heading out of the swamp.

He knew exactly where he was going. He crossed the field, plodding over clods of dirt, wading through waist-high weeds, and skirting around tangled bushes. The end of the steel mill property lay not far away and he followed its fence line to the street.

To his left, two blocks away, he could make out the house he'd grown up in. He stood and gazed in its direction a moment and then headed the opposite way. He took his time, careful not to be seen, and slipped around behind a plaza.

The narrow lane was lined with employee parking on one side, putrid dumpsters and stacks of empty skids on the other.

His destination lay dead ahead, just past a big blue bin. He crept around, opened a metal service door, and peered inside. Skids of groceries filled the large room, ready to replenish the supermarket shelves. He crept in carefully, looking up and down each aisle. No one was about. The lazy slob was probably on an extended break.

Adam moved to a small table near the wall and selected exactly what he knew was there—a box cutter, razor sharp and deadly. That would do the job nicely. He held the tool in one hand, ducked down behind a barrel, and waited.

He didn't have to wait long. Paul Patton came through the swinging doors from the main area of the supermarket, whistling a stupid tune. The guy who had bullied him for so long at school, constantly making fun of his condition, would bully him no more. Even at work, when Adam had tried to do his best to keep the parking lot free of carts, the man tortured him. Adam figured Paul had gotten the job here for that one purpose—to continue his constant harassment.

Adam licked his lips and waited until Paul turned his back, fiddling with something on a skid, and then he crept from his hiding place. He gripped the box cutter, holding it behind his back.

"Paul," he said.

Paul grunted and turned around, his eyes narrowing at the sight of Adam. "What're you doing here, you lazy slob? Shouldn't you be out there pushing buggies around?"

"I'll never push a shopping cart again," Adam said, bringing the knife from behind his back. He held it up and leered at the bully.

Paul stared back, never expecting the box cutter would slash across his face the way it did. Never expecting the second swing of Adam's arm would slit his throat.

The victim's eyes bulged as he stared at his murderer, blood soaking his shirt, and then he slowly slumped to the floor with a gurgling sound.

Adam chuckled, expertly tossed the knife onto the bench ten feet away, and then knelt beside the dying man. He watched Paul frantically gasp for air, the victim's hands at his own throat in a futile attempt to stop the bleeding. The bully's eyes glazed over and he took his last breath.

In a few seconds, it was all over. It was too easy—for Paul. After all the years of mental anguish the bully had inflicted, Adam wished he could've made him suffer a little longer. But he didn't have time. However unlikely, there was the danger someone might come into the back room. It didn't matter all that much if he was seen. He was a wanted man anyway, and one more victim didn't make any difference. But he might as well play it safe.

He stood and turned to go and then stopped; he had to do what was right. It wasn't proper to leave Paul lying there. He stooped over the fresh corpse, grabbed it by the shirt with both hands, and dragged it to the door. He rolled it outside, then went back in and mopped up the blood with paper towels. He found an industrial-sized garbage bag on a shelf by the door, smiled, and took it outside.

He tussled and tugged, and finally, got the body inside the bag and tied the end securely. Then he crouched down, heaved the bag onto his shoulder, lugged it to the dumpster, and dropped it inside. It rolled and landed on the bottom of the bin with a satisfying thump.

Yes, he'd done what was right. He'd given the bully exactly what he deserved, and in the morning, he would be given a proper burial when he was carried away with the rest of the stinking garbage and dumped with the filth and stench into a putrid landfill.

Paul Patton would be where he belonged, at home for the rest of eternity.

CHAPTER 29

Wednesday, 5:26 p.m.

ANNIE BOOTED HER computer and pulled in her chair. It occurred to her, in order to find Adam Thorburn, it would help if she understood a little more about what they were up against. Her knowledge of schizophrenia was severely lacking.

Some online research brought her vast amounts of information on the disabling brain disorder. About one per cent of people have the illness, and symptoms such as hallucinations and delusions usually start between ages sixteen and thirty. That might explain why Adam's illness was worsening, and he could expect a severe increase in symptoms in the future.

Adam's mother, as well as his doctor, had mentioned his

withdrawal from others and his difficulty holding a job. On occasion, he heard voices talking to him about a variety of subjects, sometimes ordering him to do things he wouldn't normally do. That fit right in with Annie's research, and apparently, Adam had succumbed to the demands of the voices and killed without conscience.

Hallucinations, usually involving seeing people or objects that aren't there, are common, as is paranoia. Adam's doctor stated Adam also experienced delusions of persecution, believing others were trying to harm him.

The frightening disorder is usually controlled by drugs, but in Adam's case, the drugs weren't having the desired effect. And though schizophrenics are usually no more violent than the average person, Adam also displayed sociopathic tendencies. That's what made his actions so terrifying and unpredictable, leading to the vicious murders.

She would have to expect the unexpected if she were to have any chance of narrowing in on Adam Thorburn.

Annie printed out some of the most informative web pages, stapled them together, and tucked them into a folder. She would go over them more thoroughly later, but for now, she had a pretty good picture of Adam Thorburn's illness.

She pushed back her chair, went into the kitchen, and looked through the window above the sink. Jake was kicking around a soccer ball with Matty and Kyle. Jake dove for the ball and rolled to his back, missing an expert shot into the net.

Her cell phone rang and she picked it out of a basket on the counter. She didn't recognize the phone number.

"Mrs. Lincoln? Annie Lincoln?" came from the phone after she answered the call.

"Yes. This is she."

There was a long pause, only the sound of breathing on the line. "Who is this, please?" she asked.

Another short pause, then a low voice spoke. "This is Adam Thorburn."

Annie held her breath, unsure what to say. Finally, she asked, "Adam, where are you?"

"I can't tell you that, but I'm somewhere where you'll never find me."

"We want to help you," Annie said. It wasn't really a lie, only partially. Locking him up would certainly help Adam, and others as well.

"I talked to your husband earlier," Adam said. "He told me the same thing, but I don't believe him."

"Then why're you calling?" Annie asked. "If you don't believe my husband, why would you trust me?"

"I … I'm not sure." Adam's voice was weak, almost imperceptible. "I just want to be left alone and I thought maybe—"

"The police are never going to leave you alone. You killed two people and they won't stop looking until they've found you."

"Two people?" The voice on the line had a hint of desperation and disbelief. "What do you mean, two people? Mrs. White is the only one I know about and I don't even remember that?"

"What about the janitor, Raymond Ronson?" Annie said. "You killed him at the school yesterday."

Adam took a sharp breath. "Mr. Ronson?" He breathed heavily, quickly. "I killed Mr. Ronson too? Yesterday?"

Annie couldn't be sure if the man feigned innocence, or if he actually didn't know, but he seemed genuinely shocked to hear the news.

Adam continued, his voice pleading, "Why would I hurt Mr. Ronson? He was always kind to me." He paused. "It's the voices. Sometimes they tell me to do things, then later I forget they spoke to me. Then sometimes it all comes rushing back at once and I remember certain things, but only vaguely. This has been going on a long time. You have to believe me."

"Why should I believe you, Adam?"

Adam's voice took on a note of sadness. "You don't have to. If only you understood, then you might. I have blackout periods where I do things I regret later. I can't help it."

Annie spoke soothingly. "Then give yourself up and get some help."

"I ... I can't. They'll lock me up."

"Isn't that better than killing more innocent people?"

"Perhaps," Adam said, his voice a whisper. "Perhaps it is, but I don't have the strength."

"Think about your mother, Adam. Would she want you to continue killing people?"

"No, she wouldn't, but she said I need to decide for myself. She told me to do what I think is best for me."

"And what do you think is best for you, Adam?"

"You're starting to sound like my shrink. Dr. Zalora used to ask me that a lot."

"And what did you tell him?"

Adam gave a long sigh. "I've never been faced with this before. The things I did in the past were minor compared to what I've done now."

"You must make a decision." Annie spoke firmly, but carefully. "We can get you some real help."

"There's no help. I've tried everything." He inhaled sharply and paused, then spoke low, in a hoarse voice. "I think I might've killed someone else today. It's coming back to me now."

Annie gasped. "Who?"

"I ... I don't remember. I only remember seeing blood. Lots of blood. And I had a knife in my hand. That's all I know."

"Who was it? Where did it happen? Think, Adam. Try to remember."

Adam breathed heavily for a few moments, then, "That's all I know." He paused again, then whispered, "I don't know who it was and I'm afraid."

Annie thought quickly. If Adam was being honest, then he was afraid of what he'd become, afraid of the unknown, and fearful of what might happen to him. But if he'd killed again, it would only continue and possibly become more frequent until he was caught. She had to gain his trust. She spoke calmly and quietly. "Adam, if you tell me where you are right now, I'll come to you. I'll come alone and we can talk some more."

Adam seemed to be considering her suggestion, his breathing slightly calmer now. "I wanted to give myself up before, but the voices wouldn't let me." He took a deep breath. "They told me to kill myself, and when I tried, they made me stop. They won't go away until I do exactly what they want."

"Trust me, Adam," she whispered.

"I ... I can't," he said. "I only called to ask you to leave me alone. To try to make you understand I can't give myself up. I have too much at stake."

"Other lives are at stake as well," Annie said, in a last desperate attempt.

There was silence, then Adam said, "I have to go now. I'm calling from a phone booth so don't bother trying to trace the call."

"Wait. Adam," Annie pleaded, but it was too late. There was a distinct click over the line as the killer disconnected.

She hung up thoughtfully. She'd done her best, but it was apparent to her he was never going to surrender of his own free will. She would have to notify Hank, but unfortunately, Adam had given no indication as to where he could be found.

She hurried to her desk and browsed the printouts again. Everything Adam had said fit precisely with the listed information, and was exactly as Dr. Zalora had said.

Adam was reaching out, and she felt she had failed in what might've been her only chance to stop a killer and save additional lives.

CHAPTER 30

Wednesday, 6:14 p.m.

HANK SLUMPED in his chair and stared at his desk, piled high with folders, reports, and work still vying for his attention. He felt exhausted from the long hours of interviews. Detective King had returned to the precinct some time ago, and between the two of them, they had talked to just about everyone Adam Thorburn knew. Some of Adam's classmates had moved from the city, and there were a few they couldn't track down, but he would locate them as soon as possible.

As expected, no one had seen Adam recently, and most of the people they visited took it seriously when he warned them to be vigilant until Adam was found. Hank didn't want to attend another murder scene he could've avoided by spending a little more time on the job. He knew from past experience, it paid to be thorough. Sometimes leads came from the least obvious sources.

Earlier, he arranged to have more patrols around the Thorburn residence. Officers also staked out the backyard and the front of the house, staying watchful around the clock. The officers at the rear were hidden well. They would spend the long hours sequestered in the garage, staring through a small window. Hank didn't envy them their task.

When his cell phone rang, he looked at the caller ID. It was Annie. He answered it and she told him she had some important information to share, and if he would be at the precinct for a while, she and Jake would be right over.

He assured her he would be there and hung up the phone.

Detective King wandered over and plopped into a chair, a coffee in one hand, a muffin in the other. "Thought I might call it a day," he said. "Unless you have something urgent."

Hank looked closely at King. "You have something more important to do?"

King shrugged, finished his coffee, and set the empty cup on the desk. "Not really. Just want to go home and put my feet up. It's been a long day."

"For both of us," Hank said.

King disregarded Hank's comment, downed the last bite of muffin, and stood. He waved a hand and strode away, calling over his shoulder, "See you tomorrow."

Hank frowned, dropped King's cup into the wastebasket,

blew the crumbs off the edge of his desk, and turned back to his paperwork.

He was sorting through the notes he had made during his afternoon visits when he heard a familiar voice call.

"Hey, Uncle Hank."

He pushed back his chair and swung toward the voice. "Hey, Matty," he said.

The boy moved closer and gave Hank a fist bump. "Catch any bad guys lately?"

"Working on it. There's no shortage of them out there and I'm doing my best to get my share."

Annie and Jake were close behind Matty and they settled into guest chairs. Matty wandered across the precinct floor, probably looking for a friendly cop he could pester with questions.

"So what's the important information you have for me?" Hank asked, looking back and forth between Jake and Annie.

Annie leaned forward. "I received a phone call from Adam Thorburn. On my cell phone."

Hank's mouth dropped open a moment, then he looked over his shoulder. Callaway was working late. He looked back at Annie. "You have your phone with you?" he asked, holding out a hand.

Annie removed her cell from her handbag and held it out.

"Let me see if we can find out where he called from," Hank said, taking the phone.

"It's the last inbound call," Annie said. "From an unknown name. He said he was calling from a phone booth."

"We'll find out exactly where," Hank said. He spun his

chair around and wheeled over to Callaway's desk. He handed Callaway the phone, explaining what he needed. "Can you find out where the call came from?"

"No problem, Hank," Callaway said. He took the phone, sat forward and thumbed through it, then got to work at his keyboard. "Give me a few minutes."

Hank wheeled back to his desk and looked at Annie. "How long ago did he call?"

"Just before I called you. I'm sure he didn't stick around after that."

"Nonetheless, it'll tell us what neighborhood he's hanging around," Hank said. "Now, tell me about the call. Did you record it?"

"We only record calls to the landline," Annie said. "I'm not exactly sure what he wanted. He seemed to be reaching out for help, but on the other hand, he adamantly refuses to surrender."

Hank sat back, his brow furrowed in thought. "He's a confused individual."

"When I mentioned Raymond Ronson, he seemed genuinely surprised to hear about the murder. And upset. He said Mr. Ronson was always good to him."

"At least that tells us he knew Ronson," Hank said. "That's something I was unsure of, and I believe Ronson was not a random target."

"Here's the disturbing news," Annie said. "He told me he vaguely remembers another murder today. It came back to him while he was on the phone. He claims only to remember lots of blood and a knife."

Hank leaned forward, his lips in a tight line. If what Adam had said was correct, that made three murders in three days. "He has no idea who the victim was?"

Annie shook her head. "He said he can't remember."

"There've been no reports of a murder anywhere in the city today," Hank said. "Of course, that doesn't mean much. A lot of murders go undiscovered for days, weeks sometimes."

"He also mentioned his blackout spells and voices in his head."

"Voices?"

"I did some research on schizophrenia," Annie said. "That's one of the symptoms. Voices telling you what to do. Adam said they don't stop unless he does exactly what they tell him to. Paranoia and delusions of persecution are more symptoms, and Adam is experiencing them all."

Hank nodded. "I know a bit about schizophrenia, but Adam's a sociopath, and that's what makes him dangerous." He looked up as Callaway came over and handed him a sheet of paper.

"Call came from a phone booth at Mill and Remedy Road," the technical whiz said. "I've dispatched a couple uniforms to the area, but don't hold your breath."

Hank took the paper and glanced at it. "Thanks, Callaway."

"I believe there's a plaza at Mill and Remedy," Jake said. "I've been in the area a lot in the last couple of days."

"That's the plaza where Mortino's is," Hank said. "Where Adam works."

"At least we know he's still in the neighborhood," Annie said.

Jake nodded thoughtfully. "I don't think he has plans to leave."

Hank dropped the sheet of paper on his desk, leaned back, and crossed his arms. "He's targeting people he knows, so I agree with you, Jake. I don't think he'll leave the area as long as he continues to kill. Almost everyone he knows is from around here."

"And you contacted them all?" Annie asked.

"Between King and me, everyone we could track down was notified and warned. Some have moved away, but we'll eventually find them and give them a phone call."

"In the meantime, I don't think we have any other leads," Annie said. "If Adam calls again, I'll try once more to get him to surrender, but it's unlikely."

"We have cops everywhere," Hank said. "But Thorburn is smart and he's finding a way around us." He shrugged. "But he can't keep it up forever. If he returns home again, we'll get him."

"I'm sure we will," Annie said and looked at Jake. "Shall we go?"

"I'll find Matty," Jake said. He wandered off and returned a minute later with the boy.

"See you later, Uncle Hank."

Hank waved a hand and watched his friends leave the precinct before turning back to his desk. He had a few more things to take care of, then it would be time to call it quits for another day.

He arranged to have an unmarked police car wait in the plaza and watch the phone booth Thorburn had used. He assumed the killer would know the call could be traced and wouldn't use the phone again, but he also knew even the smartest criminals slip up eventually.

Hank wanted to be ready when Thorburn made that fatal error.

CHAPTER 31

Wednesday, 6:55 p.m.

ADAM THORBURN sat on the grass, facing the swamp he loved, the rosebush an arm's length away, trying desperately to remember more details about where he'd been that afternoon. He remembered calling Annie Lincoln; that was clear in his mind. It was what had taken place earlier that concerned him most.

All he had was the memory of blood and a knife. He must've had another one of his blackout periods and done something stupid again. He remembered being in the hut thinking about Mrs. White, then going to the plaza to make a call to Annie Lincoln. Then he returned and had something to eat.

But what happened before that? Had he done another crazy thing? The memory of blood and the knife could only mean one thing. He'd killed again with no clear memory of the event. Whenever he closed his eyes, the sight came back—a knife, dripping with blood. And the weapon was in his hand. That much he knew. The memories that had come back to him while he was on the phone with Annie were true.

And what about the janitor, Mr. Ronson? Annie Lincoln told him they knew it was him, and now there was no doubt in his mind. He had killed three people and it frightened him. And having little or no memory of the events was even more terrifying.

He still wasn't sure why he'd made the phone call. There had been no voices telling him to—they were strangely silent today. Perhaps after the murder, he'd been subconsciously compelled to tell someone. The business card he'd found at the house must've planted the idea in his head.

Annie said she wanted to help him and he wondered if it were true. Not likely. She only tried to get him to surrender so they could lock him away. He dug inside his pocket and found the card, ripped it into shreds, and tossed the pieces high above his head. They floated through the still air and fluttered to the ground around him.

He shielded his eyes with a hand. Ahead of him, the early evening sun barely made it between a pair of tall trees, their branches sagging toward the black water, their roots devouring nourishment from the rich wetlands. He lay back, turned his face to the sky, and closed his eyes.

He needed to make some decisions. He could no longer

go on this way—killing, hiding, and running away. There had to be an answer somewhere. He must cling to that hope; the alternative was too terrifying. He knew what happened to people in prison, especially someone young and soft like him.

He wondered if he had known the third person he'd killed. He assumed he did; he knew the first two. Perhaps if he went east, or west, maybe even south, it would be safer for him and everyone around him. If he didn't know anyone where he went, then maybe he wouldn't kill again.

But what about his medication? Without any identification he'd never be able to get any. As bad as he was with his meds, he was much worse off without them.

Sighing deeply, he rolled to his feet and went inside the hut. The last half of the chicken was still where he'd left it, wrapped securely in the grocery bag. He undid the knot and removed the meat, spread the bag out on the floor, and laid the chicken on top. He wasn't all that hungry, but he knew he must eat to keep his strength up.

He ripped apart the carcass and frowned at a small plastic bag inside the bird. He pulled it out, unzipped it, and removed a folded piece of paper. When he flattened out the note, he recognized his mother's handwriting.

"Adam," the note began. "Meet me in the morning, Thursday, at the old Cochran house. You know where it is. It's been empty now for some time but you'll be able to get in the side door. I'll leave it open for you. I'll be waiting for you at nine. Be careful and watch out for the police. They're in the area all the time now and they're also watching my house." The note was signed, "Mother."

Adam folded the paper and laid it on the shelf. She would likely bring him some clean clothes, maybe some more food, and whatever else she thought he might need. He looked forward to seeing her, and he knew the house she mentioned, but he would have to be careful.

Food was what he needed most, and an idea came to him. If he ran low, the grocery store where he used to haul the carts around wasn't far away and he knew the place well. If he was careful, he might be able to slip in the back door and help himself to the rows and rows of food and supplies he knew were there. He would keep the idea in mind for the future should it become necessary.

He'd have to be careful and watch out for Paul Patton, though. The bully who had tortured him at school worked there, stocking shelves, but was often the only one who ventured into the storeroom. Paul was kind of dumb anyway, and it wouldn't be hard to get around him.

The more he thought about it, the better the idea sounded. But it presented a problem. He would have to go during the day when the store was open, and that increased his chances of being seen by the cops in the neighborhood. If only he could disguise himself in some way, something they would never suspect, like a woman, maybe pushing a baby carriage.

He laughed at the idea, the first time he had laughed in a while, and it made him feel better.

Then as if his rare outburst caused an eruption inside of him, in his mind, he felt himself slipping into a panic attack. He looked around fearfully. He heard them outside the hut, creeping in on him. They had him surrounded. He dashed from the hut and spun around, straining his eyes in all directions. They were well hidden, but they were coming for him. They were going to take him away and lock him up forever.

"You'll never get away," a voice said. "You have to fight for your freedom."

Then another voice. "If you hide, they'll leave. Just hide."

"No. You must bury yourself in the swamp. They'll never find you there."

Adam covered his ears, let out a roar, and fought to keep his sanity. The voices were in his head. There was no one in the swamp with him. They were inside him, torturing him, goading him on, attempting to drive him to his own destruction.

"Go, Adam. Release your pain. Go into the swamp. It'll take care of you."

"No," Adam shrieked. "No."

"You must, Adam. It's the only way. Trust me."

"Don't listen to him, Adam. Don't listen. Hide, Adam. Hide."

Adam clenched his fists, dropped his head back, and howled, "Leave me alone." He raised a fist, punching himself in the side of his head, over and over. "Get out of there. Go away."

"You must listen to me, Adam. You're injuring yourself. You're not hurting me. If you want me to go, then bring me some blood. You know where to find blood, Adam. Just one more time and I'll leave you alone. It's what you need."

"Adam, no. Don't listen. You must hide. Run and hide."

Adam roared again, then turned and dashed into the hut. He fell down on all fours, resting on his elbows, pulled the blanket over his head, and screamed. He would drown out the evil voices with his own. He wouldn't listen to them anymore. They brought him nothing but despair and pain.

He continued to scream, his mental anguish increasing, his voice growing hoarse, his lungs bursting.

And still, he screamed on.

CHAPTER 32

Wednesday, 7:21 p.m.

HANK YAWNED and snapped his briefcase closed. He had been in the habit of taking files and reports of ongoing cases home with him, and this case was no different. It continually weighed on his mind, and he never knew when a thought might strike him, often in the middle of the night.

Besides, he seemed to have a habit of working himself to sleep every evening. The anguish of victims, and the suffering of their families, became his cross to bear, and he found it hard to set a case aside when the lives of innocent people depended on him.

That commitment was to blame for his minimal social life, specifically his love life. When he'd met Amelia a few months ago, it had been a turning point. At that time, he vowed to himself he would keep his job separate from his personal life; however, he found that resolve not only difficult to keep, but impossible at times, especially when he was involved in a case like the current one.

He would have to make it up to Amelia when this was all over. He owed her that much for her undying patience and understanding. Perhaps a week or two away—far away—would be exactly what he needed. What they both needed.

Hank sighed. The problem was, she'd heard that before and the time never came. Something always got in the way. Yet she still loved him in spite of—and perhaps because of—his dedication. But for how long? He prayed he would never have to look back on this day, filled with regret because of the wonderful woman he had let slip away.

He pushed back his chair, stood, and looked around the quiet precinct. Callaway worked on. Three or four officers chatted at the watercooler, soon to be on their way home. The night shift would arrive soon, a bare skeleton remaining in the precinct, others patrolling the streets. Perhaps one of them would turn up Adam Thorburn tonight.

He picked up his briefcase, crossed the floor, and poked his head into Diego's office.

The captain sat at his desk, leaning back in his chair, absorbed in some papers. He looked up at Hank and motioned for him to come in. "Sit down a minute."

Hank stepped inside, settled into a chair, and set his briefcase on the floor beside him. "What's up, Captain?"

Diego slid the papers onto his desk, gave a long noisy

stretch, and dropped his elbows on the rests, clasping his hands in front of his rounded belly. "I've been going over what I have on the Thorburn case," Diego said. "Are you making any headway in finding this guy?"

"Some, Captain. We know he's still in the area. He had a run-in with Jake Lincoln earlier, but unfortunately, he got away."

"Lincoln? What happened? Why didn't he nab him?"

"They had a chain-link fence between them and he couldn't get at him. Jake tried to chase him, but no luck."

Diego folded his arms. "So nothing solid on Thorburn's current whereabouts?"

"Only that he's close by," Hank said. "It's just a matter of time. The public's on the lookout as well. We've fielded several calls today from people pointing us toward someone who fits Thorburn's description. Officers have checked them out, but so far, all false alarms."

Diego frowned and adjusted his cap. "How much longer can this guy elude us? I don't want any more bodies."

"It's only been two days, Captain, and we've laid a lot of groundwork. Cops all over the city are watching for him. Everyone Thorburn knows has been alerted and warned. Whether or not they take the warning seriously, I can't tell, but we've done all we can."

Diego's head bobbed up and down knowingly. "Okay, go home, Hank." Diego dismissed him with a wave. "We'll get him tomorrow."

Hank picked up his briefcase, stood, and moved toward the doorway. "I hope so, Captain. Goodnight."

"Oh, Hank."

Hank turned back.

"How's it working out between you and King?" Diego asked, stroking his mustache. "I realize he's a little rough around the edges."

Hank shrugged. "He has his uses. He lacks finesse, that's for sure, and I have to prod him from time to time, but I've pretty much learned how to handle him. He's still a slob, but I think he's gotten over some of his arrogance. Gets along with the Lincolns better now. Not sure what he had against them at first. Maybe he saw them as some kind of threat. I don't know."

Diego grunted and observed Hank closely.

"He's not such a bad cop when he gets his butt in gear. Good on the streets." Hank chuckled. "But if you're thinking of transferring him, it won't break my heart in the least."

Diego gave a short laugh. "I'm sure it wouldn't." He waved Hank out again, then leaned forward at his desk and picked up his paperwork.

Hank left the precinct, rounded the building, and got into his car. He hoped Diego was right about finding Thorburn tomorrow.

He drove from the lot, heading home. He was concerned about the third victim Thorburn claimed to have killed. Hank was keeping an eye out for any incoming reports, but no bodies had been discovered. If Thorburn was telling the truth, that made three victims in three days, and Hank dreaded what might happen tomorrow. Perhaps a fourth?

His cell phone rang; it was Teddy White again. Hank filled

him in on their latest findings and assured him they were making good headway and he would catch his wife's killer soon.

He parked in his usual spot behind his apartment building, made his way inside, and laid his briefcase on the kitchen table. After a quick snack, he would browse through the evidence again in the hopes something would jump out.

Then he would retire early. Perhaps he would be awakened in the night with the good news that Thorburn had been apprehended. If not, he would get a fresh start in the morning and do his best to stop the killings and bring the murderer to justice.

CHAPTER 33

DAY 4 - Thursday, 8:45 a.m.

ADAM THORBURN had been wide awake since the sun had come up over the tops of the thick bushes and stalwart trees surrounding his hut in the swamp. He sat outside enjoying nature, lounging on the rich, spongy grass near his rosebush. It'd been another fitful night's sleep, with only the quiet sounds of the bog to lull him into the peace he yearned for.

As much as he loved the calm tranquility of the swamp, he couldn't picture himself staying here forever. He wasn't much for social interaction, but he looked forward to a visit with his mother. Since his father died, she was the only one he could talk to—the only one he cared to talk to. Nobody else understood him like she did.

Sure, his shrink understood him, but only in a clinical way, not on a personal level. Adam suspected Dr. Zalora cared more about collecting his fees than anything else—fees his mother couldn't afford. He wasn't sure how they got by with only his occasional paycheck and her meager earnings from the bar.

He looked at his watch. It neared nine o'clock and his mother would be waiting. It would take him a few extra minutes to get there, especially now that the streets were littered with cops sure to be on the lookout for him.

He hoped that Lincoln guy wasn't around. He was big, and Adam wouldn't stand much chance against the guy's long legs. And God forbid he ever got into a physical altercation with him. He'd be toast, that's for sure. He would need to be doubly vigilant from now on.

Rising to his feet, he started off. He was deep in the swamp, but he'd been in and out of there so many times he knew exactly the best route to take. He walked across spongy ground, eased across fallen trees, and hopped over muddy areas, finally making it to the edge of the wetland.

He faced a wide open and unused field, and the steel mill beyond it. His destination was the corner house of the next street—the same street his mother's house was on. Hardly a safe zone to be venturing into, but he was confident and determined.

Crossing the field to the back of the mill's property, he strode along the fence line to the corner, then turned and headed toward the street. A car drove by as he drew closer, and he ducked down into the long weeds, waited until it was clear, and then proceeded to the sidewalk.

He was at the intersection, a block away now, with no more weeds to hide behind. He could make out the Cochran house at the end of the block. Glancing around, he studied the area and chose his path carefully. There were lots of trees to duck behind, but that's all that offered any hiding places should one be necessary during his long walk up the short block.

A police car nosed around the corner by the Cochran house and Adam dove backwards, dropped to the ground, and wormed his way into the tall weeds. He watched the car come toward him, then turn and head down the street. It was a close call, but if the cruiser rounded the block continually, Adam should have enough time before the vehicle made its next round.

Stepping back to the sidewalk, he looked in both directions. The coast was clear, at least for now. He darted across the street, kept a close eye ahead of him, and raced up the block. He jumped a hedge and landed on the grass at the rear of the Cochran house.

He crouched down to catch his breath, out of view from anyone on the street, and then looked toward the side door of the house. His mother had said it would be unlocked. He glanced at his watch; it was just past nine o'clock.

He looked toward the neighbor's house. The windows were darkened and he couldn't tell if anyone was inside. More than likely not. They probably worked at the mill, and anyone at home would be lounging in the living room.

Crossing the lawn carefully, he climbed onto the small

wooden porch and pulled on the screen door. It was unlocked. He eased it open and turned the knob on the inner door. It turned, clicked, and then squeaked as he pushed it open.

He stepped into the bare kitchen and smiled at his mother, sitting at the kitchen table, a look of relief on her face as she glanced toward him.

"Sit down, Adam," she said, motioning toward a chair.

He looked at the chair, wondering if it would hold him. Two of the others were broken, and the table was chipped and worn. It was no wonder it had been left behind when the Cochrans moved out. He dropped carefully into the only remaining solid chair and laid his arms on the table. "It's good to see you."

"I was afraid you wouldn't make it," she said, laying a hand on his. "How have you been?"

Adam shrugged. He was mentally exhausted, afraid, and uneasy about the future. "Given the circumstances, I'm doing okay," he said, forcing another smile.

"Have you been taking your medication?"

He nodded.

"I was afraid you wouldn't get my note," she said. "I assumed you'd take the roast chicken. I left it for you."

"I got it," he said, glancing around the kitchen. Newspapers littered the countertop. A green garbage bag, half full, was tossed in a corner. The room smelled musty, dirty, and long overdue for a scrubbing. "How safe is this place to meet?"

"It's safe enough," she said. "The police have already been here. I doubt if they'll come back."

"What about the owners?"

"It's been empty for a long time. It's for sale, but nobody wants to live in this neighborhood." She laughed. "It should be safe for a while."

"Maybe I could stay here sometimes. In the winter."

"If you're careful coming and going, you might be fine here," she said. "The police are watching my house all the time now, and a couple of cops are hidden in the garage. Whatever you do, don't go home."

Adam looked closely at his mother. She had taken a big chance in meeting him here. "You could get in a lot of trouble for this," he said. "Aiding and abetting a fugitive."

"You're my son," she said, as if that settled the matter.

He nodded. "But I'll have to leave the area eventually."

She looked worried at that. "I don't want you to go."

"I might have to."

"I brought you some things," she said, reaching for a bag on the table. She opened it and looked inside. "There's some more food in here, a cap, and some money."

"Thanks. I don't know how I can spend the money, but I can always use the food."

She reached into the bag, paused and looked at Adam, and then pulled out something wrapped in newspaper. "I brought you this." She pushed it across the table toward him. "You might need it."

He lifted the heavy package, then frowned, peeled back the paper, and recoiled in horror at the sight of a pistol.

"I don't want this," he said, pushing it away.

She pushed it back toward him. "Just in case," she said

soothingly. "You don't have to use it. It's only for protection."

He stared at the shiny weapon. He couldn't trust himself with it. He was dangerous enough without a gun. How much worse would he be with one?

"It's okay," she said. "I want you to be safe."

He nodded. He decided to take it with him, but if he got any crazy ideas, he would toss it deep in the swamp. He looked back at his mother, his eyes narrowing. "They said I killed Mr. Ronson." He leaned in. "Did I?"

She nodded and sighed deeply. "Yes, you did, Adam. But remember, it's not your fault."

"I don't want to kill anyone else." He rocked himself back and forth in the chair, wringing his hands, looking toward his mother for help.

She reached out and put a hand on his shoulder to calm him down. "You won't. I talked to Dr. Zalora about you, and he thinks you'll be fine now. As terrible as it was, it was something you had to get out of your system. I didn't tell him I saw you. He would have to report it if I did, so I have to be careful what I say to him."

He hoped Dr. Zalora was correct. If not, he would have the pistol, and he could always use it on himself. If he had the strength, that is.

"You'd better go now," she said. "I'll wait until you're gone before I leave."

He wrapped up the gun, dropped it into the bag with the rest of the supplies, then stood and went to his mother, giving her a hug.

She sat quietly at the table as he opened the door and stepped out. He took a last look at her, closed the door, and hurried across the lawn. He peered over the hedge to make sure the coast was clear and then hopped over, landing on the sidewalk.

He hurried cautiously up the street and scurried into the field of tall weeds. As he made his way back to the swamp, the bag weighed heavily on his arm, and the pistol it contained weighed heavily on his mind.

CHAPTER 34

Thursday, 9:37 a.m.

LISA KRUNK had been following the story of Adam Thorburn closely, and she'd managed to conduct interviews with just about everyone involved. Though she'd searched long and hard, she hadn't been able to locate Adam. An interview with him would be like gold in the bank, and her ratings would soar even higher than they already were.

An interview with Virginia Thorburn would be the next best thing, and though Lisa had tried in the past, the woman always eluded her calls and never answered Lisa's knock on the door.

Not today, though.

She needed to talk with Virginia. Lisa's viewers depended

on her expertise to keep them fully informed of the latest in breaking events. It was her determination that consistently put her stories at the top of the news.

There was only one choice—an ambush.

And luck was with her. As Don spun the van onto Mill Street and neared the Thorburn residence, Lisa spied Virginia Thorburn coming down the sidewalk.

She pointed frantically toward the woman. "Pull over, Don. That's her."

Don turned the steering wheel, touched the brakes, and the van jerked to a quick stop. His door swung open and he jumped out, opened the side door, and grabbed his camera. In one deft move the camera landed on his shoulder, the red light glared, and he was raring to go before Lisa could locate the cordless mike and climb from the van.

She smiled smugly at his eagerness. She had trained him well, and he knew every move she made, and every word she spoke, was worthy of being captured on video. And when she had a subject in her sights, he had better keep up with her. That is, if he wanted to continue getting the generous paycheck she provided him with every week.

Lisa hit the sidewalk, gripped the mike, and flicked it on. Virginia Thorburn stopped short, a frown on her face as Lisa strode toward her, Don at her side. The woman glanced around as if looking for a quick exit, then her shoulders slumped as she gave in and waited.

Lisa faked a wide smile and spoke into the microphone. "Good morning, Mrs. Thorburn." She pushed the mike at the trapped woman and waited for a reply.

Lisa received a frown in return.

"I wonder if I might ask you a few questions," Lisa said, the smile remaining on her stiff lips. "I'd like to get Adam's side of the story."

Virginia's face softened noticeably, but she remained quiet.

Lisa was used to that. It always helped to stroke their ego a little to get her subjects to loosen up, and then when their guard was down, hit them with the tough questions.

"Mrs. Thorburn, I've done some research on you and your son," Lisa lied. "Your undying dedication during some of his rougher periods must have been pretty hard on you."

Virginia Thorburn nodded. The woman was loosening up.

Lisa continued. "Other newscasts have portrayed your son as some kind of monster. I know for a fact that isn't true." She paused. "Will you tell my viewers what Adam is really like?"

Virginia opened her mouth for the first time. She appeared to be thinking as she stared at the microphone pushed under her nose. "Adam is ... a good son. He's never caused any trouble to me, and I believe the stories about him have been exaggerated."

"You believe he never killed anyone, Mrs. Thorburn?"

"I ... I didn't say that." The woman fumbled for words, probably unsure how best to defend someone Lisa knew was a true barbarian. Adam was one of the most vicious killers Lisa had ever run across, but she wasn't about to tell his mother her feelings. At least, not yet.

"I understand he has a brilliant mind," Lisa said.

"Yes, he does. He hasn't been allowed to reach his full potential. Maybe someday."

Lisa smiled inside. Adam would reach his full potential all right—in prison. If he lived long enough. She stifled her thoughts and said, "We'd like to see that."

Virginia bit her lip and remained silent.

"Perhaps if he gave himself up, things could be different," Lisa said.

"Adam has to make up his own mind about that," Mrs. Thorburn said, glancing at the camera. "Since I have no contact with him, I can't persuade him either way."

"You haven't see your son since he became a fugitive?"

Virginia shook her head. "I haven't seen him since Tuesday morning."

"How's he been surviving without some help?" Lisa asked.

"He's resourceful."

"Are you concerned he might kill someone else?"

The woman glanced away, took a slow breath, then looked at the camera, her eyes narrowed. "My son deserves a fair trial. If and when they find him, I hope the law will be unbiased."

Lisa cleared her throat. It was time to get nasty and perhaps get something interesting for the viewers. "Your son's a vicious and violent killer, Mrs. Thorburn. Surely you don't think it's right to protect him?"

Virginia Thorburn's eyes flashed and her face darkened. "You have no right to condemn him and no right to accuse me of protecting him." She leaned in, her voice becoming more frantic. "I told him to give himself up, but I can't force him to. He doesn't remember killing those people."

Lisa took a small step back. Mrs. Thorburn was angry, but

anger was good. In fact, Lisa did her best to get any emotions she could from her targets. Emotions kept people at home glued to their screens.

"Mrs. Thorburn," Lisa asked, "are you harboring Adam inside your house? Is he in there right now?"

Virginia's body stiffened at the question, a deep frown appearing on her brow. She pointed a finger across the street and scowled at Lisa. "The police are watching my house and they have searched it already." She stood back, her hands on her hips, and gave Lisa a black look. "I already told you, I haven't seen Adam."

This was getting good. Lisa had caught the woman in a blatant lie. She raised her chin and looked down her sharp nose at Virginia Thorburn. "So let me get this straight, Mrs. Thorburn. You haven't seen Adam since Tuesday morning, and he told you he didn't kill those two people." Lisa cocked her head. "How can that be? Are you telepathic? Mr. Ronson was killed on Tuesday evening."

Virginia gave Lisa a blank stare. She opened her mouth to speak and then closed it again.

"You've been meeting with your son, Mrs. Thorburn," Lisa stated flatly, moving in a step. Her tone became accusing. "How can you condone what this raging lunatic has done?"

Virginia's face reddened, her eyes firing hatred at Lisa. "This interview is over." She turned, brushed past Don, and strode up the street toward her house.

Lisa chased after her, Don hurrying behind, the camera still running. "Come back, Mrs. Thorburn," Lisa demanded.

Virginia didn't answer. She hurried up the driveway, digging her key from a pocket. She unlocked the door and turned toward Lisa, who was fast approaching, and pointed a finger. "Get off my property." The woman stepped inside the house, slamming the door behind her.

Lisa turned toward Don, drew a finger across her throat, and the red light on the camera blinked off.

"Let's go, Don," she said, striding toward the van. "We have some great footage here."

Don placed the camera carefully in the back of the van and jumped into the driver seat. Lisa climbed in the passenger side, well pleased with herself and the interview.

Of course, she would edit out the mushy stuff at the beginning of the interview. Its only purpose was to put the woman off her guard. The good stuff came later, and she would be sure to give it the treatment it deserved. Once she edited in other footage she had obtained elsewhere, her little exposé of Mrs. Thorburn was bound for the top of the news; there was no doubt.

CHAPTER 35

Thursday, 11:16 a.m.

ANNIE WORKED her way down Mill Street, talking to the Thorburns' neighbors in the off chance someone had seen Adam Thorburn in the area.

Though most of the residents were at work this time of day, she talked briefly to a handful of people who were at home for one reason or another—either didn't have a job or worked at odd hours. Thus far, her efforts had been unrewarded. Everyone she talked to knew Adam and was aware he was a fugitive, but no one had seen him recently.

She paused in front of the Thorburn house, attempting to come up with an excuse to visit Virginia Thorburn. She glanced across the street. The car parked there was unmarked, and the officer inside was out of uniform. She doubted if Adam would venture to the house, the presence of the car likely more of a deterrent than a trap.

Annie hesitated a moment, then went up the driveway to the side of the house, opened the screen door, and knocked. The door opened a crack, revealed Virginia's face, and then opened all the way.

"Good morning, Mrs. Thorburn," Annie said, smiling pleasantly.

The woman showed a faint smile.

"May I come in a moment?"

The door opened and Annie stepped inside.

Virginia motioned toward a chair as she took a seat at the table and leaned her arms on top.

Annie sat and laid her handbag on the table. "I came to talk to you about Adam. I'm rather worried about him."

The woman sighed deeply. "So am I."

Annie cleared her throat. "Adam called me on the phone yesterday," she said.

Virginia's eyes narrowed. "Why would he call you?"

"I'm not sure," Annie said, watching Mrs. Thorburn closely. "He said he killed another person but can't remember it clearly."

Virginia's mouth dropped open and her eyes grew wide, then she leaned forward. "Did he say who it was?"

"He didn't know, but he seemed to be struggling with it. Perhaps struggling with himself, looking for some help."

Virginia reached for her cigarette package, pulled out a smoke with a shaky hand, and managed to get it lit. She took a long drag, inhaling it deeply. Puffs of smoke came from her mouth as she spoke. "I don't know if anyone can help him."

"Perhaps not," Annie said. "I just wanted to let you know." She hesitated and spoke cautiously, watching the woman's face. "If Adam calls you, it might be best to try and convince him to turn himself in before anyone else gets hurt."

Virginia frowned. "Why does everyone think I talk to him?"

"Everyone?" Annie asked.

"This morning I was accosted by a newsperson. She said some cruel things about Adam and me. Accused me of harboring him."

Annie was pretty sure Mrs. Thorburn was referring to Lisa. She touched the woman's hand. "I think I know who it was. Her name's Lisa Krunk, and she lives to stir up trouble."

Virginia nodded, took another drag of her cigarette, and blew the smoke toward the ceiling. "I've seen her stories on TV, and when she came around earlier, I never let her in, but today she caught me in the street."

"I try to avoid her when I can too," Annie said. She picked up her handbag, pushed back her chair, and stood. "Mrs. Thorburn, for Adam's safety, please contact the police if you see him. I know he's your son, but it's the right thing to do."

Virginia stood without a word, dropped her cigarette in the ashtray, and followed Annie to the door. Annie stepped outside and walked to the sidewalk, leaving the woman silently staring after her.

Annie wasn't sure if she'd made any headway in

convincing Mrs. Thorburn, but she feared there would be other innocent victims.

She strode past the house next door. She had already talked to Mabel Shorn and didn't see the point of dropping in again. She continued down the street, talking to the inhabitants at some, her knocks going unanswered at others.

Finally, she reached the corner. The last house on the block had a side door facing the intersecting street. She stepped onto the porch, opened the screen door, and knocked.

There was no answer, so she rapped again, a little harder, and the door swung open with a groan.

"Hello," she called. "Is anyone home?"

There was no answer. Annie peered through the door and into the kitchen. The room seemed to be empty, void of furniture save for a broken-down table and two sturdy chairs. Trash littered the floor, and the room had a stale, unlived-in smell. The owners had moved out, and Annie wondered why the door was not only unlocked, but unlatched.

She stepped inside and reached for the doorknob to pull the door shut, calling one last time. "Is there anyone here?" She peered around the door toward the almost empty living room and decided the house was indeed unoccupied.

Except, something seemed out of place. She frowned at a crippled couch, missing one leg, pushed up against the far wall. A blanket and small pillow lay on top as if someone slept there on occasion. Was it just a homeless person seeking shelter, or was it Adam?

Curious now, she stepped into the living room and

examined her surroundings. A broken lamp with a twisted shade sat in one corner, empty boxes in another. The carpeting was stained and worn through in places, the walls and ceiling yellowed with age. Except for the new-looking blanket and pillow, the house appeared to have been vacated many months, maybe many years, ago.

She knew the police had been here earlier, and if the blanket was an indication of Adam's presence now, then he must've come since the place was searched. She looked around nervously and decided to leave. He might be here even now, and she should notify the police of the possibility.

"What're you doing here?" the voice came from behind her. Startled, she spun around and glared into the face of the man she recognized from his profile.

It was Adam Thorburn.

She looked toward the door. He sidestepped and blocked her passage. "Who're you?"

"Adam, it's Annie Lincoln," she said, attempting to speak as friendly as possible. "I ... I've been looking for you."

His frowning face relaxed slightly. "Mrs. Lincoln?" Then his frown deepened. "Why're you here? Can't you leave me alone?"

"You have to turn yourself in, Adam."

"I should never have called you."

She took a step toward him but stopped short when he held out a hand, palm toward her. "Don't come any closer. I don't trust you."

"Then let me leave and I won't come back," she said, then realized no one would fall for that line—especially someone with Adam's intelligence. She changed her tactic. "Better still, you leave, Adam. I'll wait until you're safely gone, then you know I have to call my husband."

He shook his head as one hand circled to his back. A moment later, his hand appeared again, gripping a pistol. "I can't do that," he said. He didn't look angry or vicious, only frightened and perhaps cautious.

She stared at the weapon wavering in his hand. She could tell he had rarely, if ever, held a gun before. A loaded pistol in the hands of the unpracticed can be more dangerous than in the hands of a skilled marksman. An expert will only shoot if required, but judging by the way Adam's finger shook on the trigger, he could inadvertently fire at her any moment.

She took a step backwards, bumping into the couch. He didn't move, and the weapon still wavered.

He looked toward the door, then moved back and closed it with a foot. "Come here," he said.

Annie eyed the weapon and stepped closer. She had no other choice and nowhere to run.

He took another step back and reached for a doorknob, twisted it, and swung a door open. "Downstairs," he said, flicking on a light switch. "You have to go down there until I decide what to do."

She glanced down the stairs.

"Give me your handbag."

She reluctantly slipped it off her shoulder and handed it to him.

He took the bag and raised the pistol. "Now go."

"You don't have to do this, Adam," she said.

He waved the pistol and his finger shook. "Now."

She stepped down the stairs, one at a time until she reached the bottom, and then turned around and looked up.

He stood at the top, watching her. "I'm sorry, Mrs. Lincoln. I truly am, but I told you to leave me alone."

The door closed and a lock slid shut.

She turned around and her eyes roved over the empty windowless room. Adam seemed to be in his right mind for now, but what might happen during one of his blackout periods was uncertain, and it frightened her.

CHAPTER 36

Thursday, 11:35 a.m.

JAKE WAS CONVINCED Adam Thorburn was somewhere in the immediate vicinity, close by the steel mill and the area surrounding it. After dropping Annie off on Mill Street an hour or so earlier, he had continued to patrol the adjacent streets in hopes the fugitive would make an appearance.

Occasionally, he had spied a police cruiser making its rounds, but thus far, all his attempts to locate Adam Thorburn had been unsuccessful.

He pulled the Firebird to the shoulder at the end of the steel mill property and gazed into the large area of land the mill encompassed. There were a lot of places a fugitive could hide. The ancillary buildings alone offered an abundance of possibilities.

But that wouldn't exactly be permanent. The buildings were in use, all contributing in one way or another to the running of the mill, and anyone hiding inside would be apt to be discovered at any time. As far as he knew, the police had already scoured the property, and their search had turned up nothing.

Jake gazed past the mill to the line of trees a quarter mile away. From where he sat, it appeared to be a vast forest. When he had discovered Adam in the area the previous day, the fugitive had made it to the opposite side of the chain-link fence. Perhaps he was hiding out somewhere in the forest.

He turned off the vehicle, pulled out his cell phone, and sent Annie a text message: "Checking in forest. Call me when you're done canvassing." He didn't get a reply, and he assumed she was in the middle of an interview.

Jake stepped from the vehicle and walked onto the empty land. It was a huge area, unused, likely owned by the mill should they have plans to expand. The even larger field behind the mill property also sat vacant, extending all the way to the forest. It was unlikely houses would be built so close to the mill, and he suspected the property was also destined for the mill's expansion one day.

He crossed the overgrown field and headed for the forest, wading through tall weeds, around pitted areas, and across gullies. He finally reached the tree line, and it didn't take him long to discover the band of trees was but a facade for the miles of swamp within, extending toward the horizon to his left and to his right.

The dark bog seemed impenetrable—ankle-deep mud in the most secure areas, with dismal and clouded waters thick with tall reeds, lily pads, and dying vegetation as far as he could see. It seemed unlikely anything but native swamp creatures could inhabit such a dense, overgrown portion of land.

He walked down the tree line bordering the swamp, only to find more of the same inaccessible bog. He glanced back toward the mill site. He had traversed its entire length, and yet on both sides, the wetlands stretched on endlessly.

He squinted, frowned, and strode toward a patch of weeds. They appeared to have been disturbed—broken, some trodden down. Other than an occasional loose dog, he knew of no large wildlife in this part of the country. He crouched down and examined the vegetation. Barely discernible but unmistakable, the path of injured greenery extended toward the city, and behind him, into the swampy land.

There was no doubt someone had been here recently, and Jake had a suspicion it was Adam Thorburn.

He rose to his feet and gazed toward the bog a moment before easing into the marshy land. He trod carefully on a solid piece of land jutting into the bog. He stopped. Ahead of him was nothing but mud, maybe quicksand, and further on, a pool of black water.

To his left, a fallen tree extended across the muddy area to a solid-looking piece of land. He stepped onto the log. It was slippery in places. He walked carefully, balanced precariously for several steps, then leaped onto the dry land.

From there, he skirted around the dark waters along what

appeared to be a solid footpath. Before long, the path ended, and he hopped across a patch of oozing mud onto a rock. Ahead of him was another rock, then another, then he leaped onto a patch of dark green grass. It led him deeper into the swamp, and he hoped he could remember his way back.

He followed the grassy strip for a few minutes and stopped short, dropping to a crouch. Dead ahead of him he spied a small building—a ten-by-ten hut, mounted on a handful of stalwart pillars. He listened for sounds of any human presence, but was only greeted by a bullfrog's deep voice.

He walked slowly toward the hut, careful to avoid fallen branches or loose vegetation. Ten feet short of the building, he crouched down beside a rosebush. To him, it looked like the same type of bush that grew along the rear of the Thorburn house. Adam Thorburn must have planted it there. Jake was on the right track, and he was sure now—this was where the fugitive was hiding out.

But was Adam Thorburn there now?

There was only one way to find out. There was no window in the side of the hut he faced, nor at the back. He crept forward, rounded the corner, and saw an undersized door with no knob, only a metal latch, a short, leather strap for a handle. He kept going. The far side of the building had a small hole cut in the wall to serve as a window.

Crouching down, he crept to the window and stopped underneath it. He listened intently for a few moments, then slowly raised his head. There was no one in the rustic one-room building.

Moving back to the door, he lifted the latch, swung it open, and stepped inside. The room was vacant save for an empty plastic grocery bag on a built-in shelf, along with bits of folded newspaper littering the floor. He examined the paper. It was from yesterday; Adam had been here recently.

But where was he now, and would he come back?

He pulled out his cell phone. No coverage. He tucked it away, stepped outside, and examined the immediate area. There was no indication of a trail other than the path he had come in on.

He picked his way back slowly, stopping once or twice to recall the proper route, and soon exited at the tree line. He tried his cell again. Three bars. He dialed Annie's number and waited, then frowned at the message: "Caller unavailable."

Why would she turn her phone off? He checked his messages and was informed she hadn't received his last text. That didn't make a lot of sense.

He put his phone away and worked his way across the field, passed the steel mill, and exited onto the sidewalk along Steel Road. His car was at the other end of the block, and he tried to reach Annie's phone again as he strode up the sidewalk. There was still no answer and his concern grew.

Reaching his vehicle, he climbed inside, hoping there was a simple explanation for his inability to reach his wife. He started the car and drove around the block, from Steel Road to Mill Street and back again, peering at each house with hopes of seeing Annie at the door interviewing the owner.

Perhaps she had moved onto an adjoining street. He checked the surrounding areas, rounding block after block, but she was nowhere to be seen. As he continued to patrol the neighborhood, he checked his phone constantly. A deep unease gnawed at him, a fear something had happened to Annie.

There was only one thing to do; he would have to retrace her route. He would start at the beginning of the street, talk with anyone who was home, and work his way to the end of the block and around to the next, if necessary.

He parked the Firebird at one end of the street, stepped out, and began his long search for Annie.

CHAPTER 37

Thursday, 11:54 a.m.

ADAM THORBURN was concerned for his safety. He was getting in deeper and deeper, with everything becoming more and more complicated.

Not only did he have Annie Lincoln locked in the basement of the house, but a few minutes ago, as he'd set out for the hut in the swamp, he had seen Jake Lincoln heading his way, coming through the fields from the bog.

Had the investigator discovered his hideout? As he ducked down behind a bush and watched Jake come toward him, the look on the big guy's face told him he had. Before long, the Firebird circled the block, no doubt looking for him.

And now, as Adam sat at the kitchen table, his head in his

hands, he had no idea what to do. He might be safe in the abandoned house for now, but how long would it be before they knocked the door down, and perhaps shot him dead like the dog he was? Maybe that would be for the best, anyway.

He stood and walked into the living room, pacing the soiled carpet silently. Annie had been banging at the door and calling his name earlier, but she had given up when he didn't answer. He had remained as quiet as possible, and she'd likely assumed he had left the house. He didn't want to hear her voice right now.

Not that he disliked her. Not at all. She was the only one who showed any compassion toward him. Whether or not she was sincere he didn't know, but he liked her nonetheless and didn't intend her any harm. But he also needed to keep himself safe from being captured, and the only way to do that, at least for now, was to confine her to the basement.

He lay on the couch and covered his head with the blanket, suddenly overtaken by fear. He shook uncontrollably for a few minutes, his breathing shallow and rapid. When the attack subsided, he wiped away the beads of sweat that had gathered on his brow and wished he were dead.

Reaching behind his back, he removed the pistol, turning it over and over in his hands. Just one shot—it would be so easy, and then his anguish would be over.

He held the pistol to his temple and put a shaking finger on the trigger. Just one shot. Do it. DO IT!

His whole hand trembled as he gripped the pistol and gritted his teeth.

"Pull the trigger, Adam."

"No, Adam. Put the gun down."

He held his breath, closed his eyes, and his finger tightened on the trigger, his mind consumed by the inner battle. The power of his will against a trembling hand.

"The only way to find true peace is to put a bullet in your brain. You must pull the trigger, Adam."

"No, Adam, no. There's still hope."

"It's the only way out. Trust me, Adam. Pull the trigger."

"No. Stop. Put the gun down."

Adam dropped his head and wept, his pistol hand falling to his side, the weapon slipping to the floor. He wiped away the tears with the back of his hand and stood, raised both fists above his head, and opened his mouth to scream. But no sound came out, and he collapsed to the floor, emotionally exhausted.

Soon, he stirred and opened his eyes. The weapon lay inches from his face, and he cursed his lack of inner strength and wished he'd never been born. He was a blight on society, not worthy of life, and too weak to do what needed to be done.

Reaching out wearily, he picked up the weapon and stood to his feet, tucking the gun behind his belt. There had to be an easier way. Some means to end it all without having to do it himself—he had no courage, no spine, and no guts to do the job.

Maybe if he made his way to the police station, he could barge in, his gun blazing, and let the cops fill him full of holes. That would surely be a way out, and it wouldn't take a lot of willpower. But then, knowing his luck, something would go wrong, and he would live through it, probably spending the rest of his life in prison confined to a wheelchair—or worse, staring at the ceiling half-paralyzed.

No, that wasn't the answer. If he found a way, it would have to be certain and final, with no margin of error.

He turned and looked through the front window toward the street. He longed to be out in the fresh air, on his own, but his home in the swamp had been discovered, and there was no other safe place he could go.

He took a sudden, sharp breath and ducked down. Jake Lincoln was coming up the sidewalk. Had he discovered him? Was he checking all the houses on the street?

Adam looked around desperately, then raced into the kitchen, dove to the side door, and spun the lock. He ran back to the living room and huddled in a corner, holding his breath.

In a few moments, a knocking sounded at the side door. He waited in fear, hardly daring to breathe. There was another knock, then an extended silence, and he breathed again.

He crept to the side door and looked out cautiously. He could see the big man's back as he moved up the sidewalk, rounding the block, heading toward Steel Road. It was a closer call than he expected, and he was in danger because of Annie. But he couldn't let her go yet. Not until he figured a way out of his dire situation—whether dead or alive, he didn't care, as long as he wasn't captured and imprisoned.

Emotionally drained, he went into the bathroom and doused his head with water. He stared at himself in the mirror, letting the cool water drip down his face. He'd lost a little weight, his face becoming gaunt, a dark shadowing under his eyes. He sighed and wiped his face on his sleeve. He didn't even have a toothbrush, but at least he could take a shower. Living in the house would've been ideal, but it was no longer a viable option—just one more thing he'd messed up.

He wandered back to the living room and looked out the window. From outside, anyone passing by could see right into the room. He didn't dare cover the window with a blanket or sheet. Someone in the area would be sure to notice a difference; the house had been vacant so long. He would have to be careful; he could've easily been seen by Jake Lincoln earlier.

He maneuvered the couch across the floor, away from its spot under the front window, and dropped down onto it. At least the electricity was still on; he didn't expect it would be disconnected. The owners had to maintain some heat in the winter or the water in the pipes could freeze and, over a period of years, the floors might buckle. That was a good thing, but he would have to be careful not to use the power often or the owners would notice it on their invoice.

Annie was being strangely silent. She no longer knocked on the basement door or called his name. There were no windows in the basement, so there was no way out other than the door. Perhaps she assumed he was gone from the house and was waiting for him to return. She wasn't in any danger down there, and he expected she knew that. He had made it clear he meant her no harm.

He would be sure to check on her later, maybe bring her some food and water. It was the least he could do. But in the meantime, he had some thinking to do. If he didn't come up with a plan soon, he would be discovered and put in the place he dreaded the most—behind bars.

CHAPTER 38

Thursday, 12:15 p.m.

HANK HAD SPENT the morning tracking down the rest of
the people who knew Adam Thorburn. It was a near success,
with only three or four eluding his search. Hank warned each
one he reached to be on their guard; however, no further
information to aid him in his pursuit of the fugitive had been
forthcoming.

Earlier, Captain Diego had notified Hank the press was
itching for an official statement. Officers were busy fielding
calls from a fearful public demanding the killer be stopped,
and the mayor was leaning on the captain to bring an end to
the situation immediately.

Diego had scheduled a news conference for 12:30, the

press had been notified, and the pressure Hank felt was temporarily relieved. But inwardly, he took it hard. His heart ached for the families of the victims, and the increasing anger he always felt in situations like this was something he found impossible to overcome.

He slid a blank piece of paper in front of him, leaned in, and picked up a pen. He didn't have a lot he could share at the moment, but he wrote down pointers to a half dozen things he would touch on, his chief concern being to alleviate the fears of the public. He tucked the notes into a file folder and went to Diego's office. The captain was on the phone, and he hung up when Hank stepped inside.

"All ready, Captain."

Diego nodded and pushed back from his desk. "Lead the way, Hank."

Hank paused in front of the doors leading from the precinct. The press had gathered in full force, many of them arriving some time ago, all anticipating the latest news they could pass on to the public.

News vans and reporters' vehicles lined the street, microphones and cameras were fine-tuned, and questions were devised and perfected. Several curious onlookers stood nearby wondering what the fuss was all about.

For much of the press, reporting the latest shocking news was about ratings, market share, or making a name for themselves. For Hank, it was personal. Not only was his professional future continually on the line, but it was his bound duty to bring a murderer to justice, a responsibility he took seriously.

Hank stepped aside and glanced at Diego. The captain nodded, straightened his tie, and pushed the door open. Hank followed him down the steps and approached the make-shift podium, covered with microphones. Diego stood to one side as Hank placed his folder on the stand, flipped it open, and cleared his throat.

"Thank you all for coming. I'll make a brief statement and then take your questions."

Hank's eyes scanned the crowd. He recalled most of the faces, the most recognizable being Lisa Krunk, in her usual spot at the front of the group, Don at her side. She caught his eye and nodded at him as if there were some big secret between them. Lisa always considered herself leader of the pack, worthy of special recognition in some way Hank didn't understand.

He continued, "As you're almost certainly aware, this past Monday evening, a woman, Mrs. Nina White, was brutally murdered. The identity of a suspect immediately became apparent. He has thus far eluded us, and we believe he struck again on Tuesday evening when Mr. Raymond Ronson was murdered."

The gathered group looked bored. They already knew everything Hank had said, and they seemed to be anticipating some new information. Hank continued, "I want to assure the public we're getting close to catching this individual before he kills another innocent citizen."

Hank held up a picture of Adam Thorburn. "I'll be distributing this photo to all of you, but I urge the public, if you see this man, please call 9-1-1 immediately. Do not try to apprehend him as he might be armed and is certainly dangerous."

He paused, closed the folder, and looked back up. "I'll take your questions now."

All hands shot up. Hank pointed to a reporter in the second row.

"Detective Corning, why is it taking you so long to apprehend Thorburn?"

"It's only been three days and the city offers a lot of places for a fugitive to hide. We're confident he'll surface soon. He'll need food, and he's on some medication he won't be able to obtain on his own. And we're following up certain leads we believe will track him down before long."

Hank pointed to another reporter.

"Considering both murders have taken place in schools, what precautions have been used to safeguard our children?"

"The schools are on lockdown during the day with armed guards watching over our kids. The buildings are patrolled in the evenings and overnight. But we can't assume Thorburn's next victim will be at a school. It could be anyone at any time." Hank paused. "I don't want to alarm anyone unduly, but please be on your guard."

Hank pointed to Lisa Krunk, uncharacteristically waiting patiently.

"Detective, will you tell me to what extent Lincoln Investigations is involved in this?"

"The Lincolns have been hired by a private individual and I can't speak for them. They're conducting a parallel investigation. They're not working for the police, though their goal is the same as ours, and they willingly share any and all information they receive with us."

Lisa persisted, "Do you think Adam Thorburn will strike again?"

"That's an unknown factor and we have to assume he may. We're taking every precaution and have warned potential victims." Hank paused. He didn't want to mention the third killing until he had some solid information. Without knowing the identity of the victim, it would serve no purpose. "There'll be no more questions, but I want to repeat my warning; please be cautious, don't go out alone at night, and keep your doors locked at all times until we have Thorburn in custody."

Hank picked up the folder and turned away as reporters continued to call out questions. Diego joined him and they climbed the steps and went into the precinct.

Hank didn't feel he had given the people anything new, but he hoped his warning to be careful would be heeded.

Diego turned to Hank. "Do you need some more help on this? I can give you all the officers you want."

Hank shook his head. "It's not the manpower that's the problem, Captain. It's the lack of viable leads that's slowing us down."

"Let me know if you need anything," Diego said, turning away and going into his office.

Hank went back to his desk, pulled up his chair, and dropped his notes from the press conference into the wastebasket. He slid the big stack of evidence in front of him and painstakingly went through everything once again.

So far, the body of the third victim hadn't been discovered, and there was a distinct possibility it might be one of Thorburn's acquaintances Hank and King had been unable to track down.

He turned his head toward King's desk. The detective had a couple of things to do and wasn't in yet. When King showed up, Hank would go over the names of the people they had contacted and make a list of those they had been unable to reach. The third victim might be one of them.

It was next to impossible to determine everyone Thorburn had come into contact with during his life, and there was always the chance the latest victim was someone who knew Thorburn—someone Hank was unaware of. He hoped his warning to the public would cover the ones they missed.

And he was worried. There were three victims in three days and today was the fourth day. Would there be another killing, and if so, what could be done to stop it? Who and where would Thorburn hit next? Both known murders were exceptionally brutal, one victim run over repeatedly by a car, the other stabbed to death with a screwdriver, and he feared the third, and perhaps the fourth, would be no different.

So far, the surveillance at the Thorburn house had netted nothing. Thorburn hadn't shown up at the phone booth again, and the officers on the streets, as well as the public, hadn't turned up a solid lead.

Until some new information came to light, there was little else he could do at the moment except review what they already knew in the hopes something might add up.

CHAPTER 39

Thursday, 12:39 p.m.

ANNIE HAD SEARCHED the basement thoroughly, looking for anything to help her break the door down, but had been unsuccessful. The room was bare except for a bag of garbage tossed into a corner. The only window was boarded over, nailed firmly, and though Annie had spent some time working at the boards, it was futile.

Her banging at the basement door, and her calls to Adam Thorburn, had gone unanswered, and she wasn't sure whether or not he was still in the house.

Though the room was cool, it wasn't damp, and the dry, stale smell was not overpowering. She'd been in worse situations before, but this time there seemed to be no way out on her own. She was at the mercy of Adam Thorburn and could only wait patiently until he released her or she was found.

She sat on the dusty floor, her back against the cool concrete wall, her knees drawn up, her attempts to escape exhausted. She had no doubt Jake was searching for her, especially since any phone calls to her number would go unanswered.

She raised her head and gazed toward the stairs at the sound of the lock being drawn back. Someone was coming, and it could only be Adam.

Rising to her feet, she waited. The door squeaked open and a pair of legs came into view. It was her captor. He descended a few steps, ducked down as if to assure himself he wasn't being ambushed, and then came down the steps, his eyes on her continually.

He carried a plastic bottle of water in his hand and he stopped a few feet away. "I brought you something to drink," he said, tossing it to her.

"Thank you," she said, catching it in one hand. She hadn't realized until now how thirsty she was, and she screwed the cap off and downed most of the cool liquid as he watched her, his arms crossed.

She held the bottle in her hand and looked at him, calculating her chances at trying to overpower him. She quickly gave up on the thought. He was at least five inches taller and outweighed her by fifty pounds.

Suddenly, as if it were an afterthought, he reached behind his back and produced the pistol. Annie stared at the weapon.

Had she misjudged him? Did he have plans to use the gun on her?

"I wish you could've left me alone," he said, holding the weapon in one hand, his arm at his side, the barrel pointed toward the floor.

Annie's gaze moved to the eyes of the killer. She didn't see murder in them. There was no coldness like she had seen in brutal killers in the past. Rather, his eyes were filled with a sadness she couldn't understand.

"What do you plan to do?" she asked carefully.

He raised the pistol and looked at it a moment, then dropped his hand again. He shook his head slowly. "I don't know. I don't know what to do."

"You could let me go," she said, hope in her voice, but doubt in her heart.

His lips were tight and grim. "I can't do that." He glanced around the room, his eyes finally resting back on hers. "Are you warm enough?"

"I'm fine," Annie said.

He tilted his head. "May I ask you a question?"

"Shoot," she said. "Uh … I mean, go ahead."

He smiled slightly at her slip-up, then said, "Why're you so kind to me? After what I've done? I've killed three people, maybe even more for all I know, and yet you don't seem to be afraid. Not only that, but if you're telling the truth, you're the only person who truly wants to help me."

"Maybe because I'm a mother," she said, wondering if she should continue. "I have a young boy, and if he was in your situation, I'd want to do everything I could to help him."

236

Adam nodded slowly, then asked, "And your husband? Is he like you? He seems to be rather angry."

"That's because you don't know him," Annie said. "If you did, you would see he's a compassionate man."

"I bet he's a good father, too," Adam said, a note of bitterness in his voice.

"Yes, he is," she said, and paused. "Tell me about your father."

Adam's shoulders slumped and he gazed over her head, unseeing, his mind in thought. Finally, he said, "My father has been dead now for almost a year. He was okay, but he never understood me. Always pushing me to be what he wanted and wouldn't accept my illness. Thought I was putting it on." He sighed. "When I dropped out of school, he tried to get me a job at the mill, but I couldn't work there."

"Why?" Annie asked.

"Couldn't concentrate on anything that long." He laughed. "I'm a pathetic excuse for a human being, I know, but that's the way I am."

"I don't think you're pathetic."

"How can you not? I've killed people. Murdered them in cold blood. People I liked. I think that makes me very pathetic indeed."

Annie had no answer for that.

"And I like you," he continued. "Does that mean I might kill you too?"

Annie's gaze moved to the weapon held at his side, his finger firmly on the trigger.

"I can't help it," he said. "Sometimes I have a desire to

kill. I hear voices in my head, demanding I do evil things, and I have to listen or they won't leave me alone."

"Do you hear them now?" Annie asked.

He shook his head. "No, but I did earlier today."

"What did they tell you?"

"To kill myself. But I couldn't do it."

"Then you have the power to resist," Annie said.

He dropped his head and sighed. "Sometimes." When he raised his head again, his eyes were sad. "But it's not only the voices. It's my blackout spells. Periods of time when I've no idea what I've done. I only know it was something terrible."

"How often does it happen?"

The sadness remained in his eyes. "Seems like every day now. It started after my father died, and it's been getting worse lately."

"You need to get some help," Annie said gently, compassionately.

"There's no help. My medications don't do anything anymore." He laughed out of self-pity. "Besides, I'm not a priority. I'm a murderer and no one is going to care about me getting any kind of help when there are more deserving people out there who don't kill."

He had a point, and she knew Adam was intelligent enough not to get taken in by any false promises she might make. She understood why he didn't want to surrender. The best he could expect was to be confined to a psychiatric facility with a constant stream of medication to keep him docile for the rest of his life.

"There's no future for me," he said. "And no easy way out."

Annie pointed toward the weapon in his hand. "Do you think that's the answer?"

He shrugged. "Maybe. Maybe not. But for now, it'll keep me safe until I decide what to do."

He glanced around the room, tears welling up in his eyes. Then he turned abruptly and strode toward the stairs. "I have to keep you here for now," he said, and then turned and plodded up the steps, tucking the pistol back behind his belt as he went.

The door closed, the lock slid shut, and she was alone again. She was unsure if she was safe, or if his dark side would take over and come back.

Annie was at the mercy of an unpredictable and dangerous man, a man out of control, and she had no way out.

CHAPTER 40

Thursday, 12:51 p.m.

JAKE HAD KNOCKED on every door on Mill Street, and in each case where someone was home, he'd been informed Annie had been there earlier, asked a few questions, and then moved on. He was no further ahead in the search for his wife than he was an hour ago. In addition, she still wasn't answering her cell phone and his text messages were ignored.

He went back to his car, circled the surrounding streets again, and then parked on Mill Street at the spot where he had dropped Annie off. He hoped she would return on her own with a simple explanation, but he knew in his heart something was very wrong.

His cell phone rang. He prayed it was Annie and was disappointed when he looked at the caller ID. It was Lisa Krunk.

"I don't have time to talk to you now," he said. "I'm in the middle of something that can't wait."

Lisa's voice came over the line. "As you know, Jake, in the past, I've always tried to help law enforcement whenever possible."

What was she getting at? She rarely did anything to help unless there was something in it for her.

"What do you want, Lisa?" Jake asked, trying to remain patient.

She paused, probably for dramatic effect. "I have some information you might find helpful."

"Helpful in what way?"

"To find Adam Thorburn."

Jake sat forward. "I'm listening."

"I had the pleasure this morning of interviewing Virginia Thorburn."

Jake shook his head in disgust. "Will you get to the point, Lisa?"

Lisa gave a long, drawn-out and exaggerated sigh. "In fact, if I hadn't caught her in the street, I doubt I would've gotten a word from her. She wasn't all that happy to see me."

That statement didn't surprise Jake. Rare was the time when anyone was pleased to see Lisa. Her expertise in bringing out the negative in the people she interviewed was well known by those who had been subjected to her questions.

"What do you have for me, Lisa?" Jake asked, his patience slipping away.

"I want to interview you and Annie when this is all over. Would you do me that favor, Jake?"

There it was. Her demands. They weren't unreasonable, but there always had to be something; her conscience never came into play.

"If it helps me find Annie, you've got a deal," Jake said.

"Annie's missing?" Lisa asked in her usual way of faking concern. "How long has she been gone?"

Jake bit his tongue. He hadn't meant to let that out, especially to Lisa. "I haven't been able to reach her on the phone," he said. "But I'm sure she's okay."

There was a short pause on the line and then Lisa spoke again. "In my attempt to get at the truth, I was able to dig out an important bit of information from Mrs. Thorburn."

Jake's patience was expended. "What did you find, Lisa?"

"It seems Virginia Thorburn has been meeting up with Adam on more than one occasion, the last time perhaps as recently as this morning. I caught her in a lie when she said she hadn't seen him since Tuesday morning—"

Jake interrupted. "Are you sure?"

"I'm sure. Apparently, Adam told her he didn't kill the two people, but he killed the second one on Tuesday evening." Lisa chuckled, well pleased with herself. "She was flustered and stormed away after she let that slip. I want to use it in my news story this evening, but I thought you should know."

"If it helps us locate Adam Thorburn, then you'll get the interview."

"And one more thing."

Jake sighed. "What is it?"

"Will you ask Detective Corning if he'll sit in on the interview?"

"I can't speak for him, but all right, I'll ask him. No guarantee on that one."

"Thanks, Jake. I knew I could depend on you."

The line went dead and Jake hung up thoughtfully. He knew Adam had been home the day before, when he'd seen him coming from the basement window and chased him across the yard of the steel mill. But it was doubtful Adam had seen his mother at that time, or he would've left through the door.

The rosebush Jake had seen near the hut in the swamp was further proof Adam had been home more than once.

He believed Mrs. Thorburn knew more than she was letting on. Why else would Adam have fled the house the day after the first murder—after spending the night at home? The only one who could've told him the police were on his trail was his mother.

She was protecting her son, which was understandable, but in the process she might be putting more lives in danger. If what Lisa had said was true, and she had no reason to lie about it, then he needed to have another talk with Virginia Thorburn.

He started the Firebird and drove up the street, stopping in front of the Thorburn house. The unmarked car still sat across the street from the dwelling, not a fun job for the officers inside the vehicle.

He stepped from the car, approached the side of the house, and knocked on the screen door.

Virginia Thorburn peeked through the window of the door, her face contorting into a frown when she saw him. Jake was sure she wasn't going to let him in, but a moment later the inner door swung open.

Jake tugged on the screen door. "Good afternoon, Mrs. Thorburn. May I speak with you a moment?"

"What about?" the woman asked, folding her arms and leaning against the door frame. She wasn't going to invite him in this time, that much was evident.

Jake glanced past the woman, hoping to see Annie inside. She wasn't, of course, and as he stood one step down from the doorway, he was still two inches taller than the woman. Jake looked down into her eyes and studied her face. "I'm looking for my wife. Did she drop in to see you today?"

Mrs. Thorburn nodded. "She was here a couple of hours ago."

Her eyes told him she was telling the truth. "Have you seen Adam today?" he asked bluntly.

She hesitated, fumbling for an answer, then, "No, I haven't seen him. I don't believe he's around here anymore."

Jake saw the lie in her eyes. Lisa Krunk had been correct. "Where is he, Mrs. Thorburn?"

"I ... I don't know." She frowned deeply. "I told you I haven't seen him."

Jake narrowed his eyes. "If you do, tell him I'm looking for Annie and I'm coming for him."

Her eyes told him everything he needed to know except

where his wife was. This time a hint of fear showed on her face, then anger. "I haven't seem Adam and I don't know where your wife is."

"Mrs. Thorburn," Jake said, "you can get into a lot of trouble for harboring a fugitive." Jake motioned toward the kitchen. "Is he here now?"

"No, he's not here?"

"Is my wife here?"

She took a deep breath and let it out in a long-suffering sigh. "Your wife's not here." She stepped back and reached for the doorknob.

Jake held the door from closing. "Don't forget," he said. "Make sure you tell him I'm coming for him and he'd better be careful." He moved his hand from the door and it slammed in his face.

He stepped down off the porch, allowing the screen door to swing closed, then made his way back to the Firebird. He got inside, tried Annie's cell in vain, and then started the car.

He could be fairly certain neither Annie nor Adam was in the Thorburn house. The cops at the road, or the ones in the garage, would've seen him for sure, and Adam wasn't that careless.

There was no doubt Virginia Thorburn was lying to him about something. The only reason she would lie is because she was protecting her son. Jake believed she knew exactly where he was hiding out. And if Annie was in the clutches of the madman and Mrs. Thorburn knew about it, she would be in a whole lot of trouble if anything happened to his wife.

If his message to Adam alarmed her, then she would be

sure to contact her son. Jake knew Adam didn't have a phone—at least not one in his own name. But whether in person or by phone, Jake couldn't be sure, but one way or another, she would deliver his message.

And he would wait until she did.

CHAPTER 41

Thursday, 1:06 p.m.

ADAM THORBURN let the steaming water cascade over his head and run down his body. It seemed like a long time since he had taken a shower, and the hot water felt relaxing as it washed away his stress. He would have to be careful not to use too much for fear of getting caught. That is, if he stayed here. Right now, he was uncertain what he was going to do. All his plans seemed to get thoroughly messed up.

He shut off the shower and stood still a moment, his eyes closed, taking deep breaths to further calm his anxiety, then stepped from the shower and picked up a cloth he had found in the kitchen. It looked fairly clean, and he used it to dry off before hanging it carefully on the curtain rod to dry out.

His clothes were stained, but clean enough until he could get some fresh ones or get the current ones washed. Maybe he would scrub them in the tub before he went to bed and let them dry overnight. His socks especially. They were kind of grimy, and he hated pulling them on again after his shower.

After getting dressed, he picked up the pistol from the vanity, looked at it, and sighed. He hated the thing, but for now at least, it was a necessary evil. He tucked it behind his belt and pulled his shirt over top.

He went out to the living room, lay on the couch, and curled up under the blanket. But the peace he had found in the shower was short-lived. All his miseries came rushing back—Annie in the basement, his unknown future, and the people he had murdered in cold blood.

His anxiety grew by the second, and he shook with fear, anger, and emotional turmoil. He stood and paced the floor but couldn't contain his anguish. It was overpowering him again and he was terrified the voices would return.

Dashing to the bathroom, he found his medication in the cabinet where he had been careful to store it. He popped two pills, one of each, and helped them down with cold water from the tap. He looked at the half-full bottles. He was depending on them more and more, and what little good they did was only temporary.

He put the pills in the cabinet, went back to the living room, and lay down again. He realized now, he would be caught eventually. There didn't seem to be any doubt about that. His life had been ruined by others. Since he was young, he'd been taunted, tortured, and teased beyond what anyone should have to endure.

"You must get rid of Annie, Adam. You must kill her now."

"No, Adam. It's not her fault."

"Kill her, Adam. Use the pistol. She's putting you in danger."

"No, Adam. No. She's the only one who cares what happens to you."

"Kill her, Adam. Shoot her, then run as far away as you can. Trust me, Adam."

Adam rolled off the couch, stumbled to his feet, and threw his head back. "Leave me alone," he howled, covering his ears. "Leave me alone."

The voices subsided but his anger remained. His life was a living hell and no one understood. No one knew the agony he went through each day to survive. No one knew the torment inflicted on him every waking moment.

He paced the floor, enraged, his hatred increasing. Then he stopped abruptly, an idea growing in his mind. He smiled grimly and pulled out the pistol. He hadn't fired it yet but figured it couldn't be too hard to get the hang of it. He found the safety, made sure it was on, then popped out the cartridge. There was more than enough ammunition for his purpose. He worked the cartridge back in and eased the weapon in behind his belt.

He strode to the kitchen, found the cap his mother had brought him, and pulled it low over his eyes. After making sure no one was on the sidewalk, he crept out the door.

He would have to be extra attentive. With all the police in the area, and Jake Lincoln nosing around, people would be on their guard, watching for him.

He kept the hat low and turned his head when he passed a house—someone might happen to be looking out the window at the wrong time. He crossed the street to avoid a pedestrian, ducked behind trees when necessary, and gradually worked his way toward his destination, four long blocks away.

Richdale Plaza was in the heart of this working-class community, a strip of stores that served the surrounding neighborhood. He'd had a short-lived job in one of the stores awhile back, delivering pizza on a broken-down bicycle to cheapskates who had no idea what a tip was. The rat-infested establishment was called Richdale Pizza, and that's exactly where he was headed now.

He slipped around the end of the building, made his way toward the service alleyway at the rear of the units, went halfway down the alley, and stopped in front of a hand-painted wooden door. A sign on the door read, "Richdale Pizza. Employees Only."

He'd been in and out of that door too many times on his delivery treks, and he knew it was the door the delivery boys used when coming and going.

He also knew the bicycle leaning up against the slimy blue bin near the door belonged to Ira Toddle. Ira Toddle—the former star of the football team, the biggest boaster at school, and the dumbest cluck Adam had ever seen. He was the most popular guy who never went anywhere, his once muscular body now turned to fat, disgusting mush.

And he was a bully.

Adam removed the pistol from behind his belt, flicked off the safety, and crouched down behind the bin. There was always somebody ordering pizza from this crummy place, and with only one delivery boy, he knew he wouldn't have to wait long.

Sure enough, less than ten minutes later, the door creaked open. Adam stood, tightened his finger on the trigger, and peered around the bin. He grinned and put his pistol hand behind his back.

Ira Toddle was coming through the door, balancing an insulated pizza bag in one palm. Unfortunately, the unknown customer was not destined to have pizza for lunch today.

That is, unless they found another delivery boy real soon.

Ira fastened the bag to the back of the bicycle and then spun around when Adam stepped out from behind the bin and called his name.

"Ira."

Ira frowned, his eyes almost disappearing into his fat face. "What're you doing here, Thorbrain? Shouldn't you be cleaning out sewers or something?"

"All finished for the day," Adam said. "I dumped all the crap on your front lawn. You can swim in it after work."

Ira took a step ahead, hunched his shoulders forward, and glared. "You watch your mouth or I'll rip you apart, you little freak."

Adam grinned and brought his gun hand around, pushing

the pistol forward until the barrel almost touched Ira's nose. "Who's a freak, Toddle?"

Ira stepped back and raised his hands halfway up, his wide eyes on the weapon. "I ... I didn't mean anything by it, Adam. I'm just joking around."

"I'm not," Adam said.

Ira swallowed hard. "I ... I'm sorry."

"Too late for that, Toddle."

"Please," the bully whined. "Put ... put the gun down."

"You're not such a big shot now, are you, Ira Toddle?"

Toddle shook his head vigorously and tried to speak, choking out something unintelligible.

Adam gritted his teeth and squeezed the trigger. The resulting explosion startled him. He hadn't expected such a big bang. The only thing he'd expected was to see a hole above Ira Toddle's nose, and that's exactly what he saw.

Adam stared at the hole, watched Ira's eyes roll up, listened to the bully's last breath escape his lips, and then lowered the weapon as Ira folded to the pavement.

He looked around, wondering if anyone had heard the shot. It was pretty loud.

He scratched his head. He couldn't leave the body here, but he would never be able to lift the fat pig into the bin.

Adam put the weapon behind his belt, bent over, and grabbed the corpse by the feet. With much difficulty, he dragged the overweight slob's body across the lane and deposited it behind a parked car that looked like it'd been there awhile.

He stood and glanced around. Satisfied no one was

coming to see what the noise was all about, he strolled down the alleyway to the street and worked his way back to his hideout, careful not to be seen.

Mentally exhausted, he lay on the couch, covered up with the blanket, and fell asleep, well pleased with his accomplishment.

CHAPTER 42

Thursday, 1:44 p.m.

ANNIE WAS TIRED of sitting on the hard floor, weary from pacing, and exhausted from trying to find a way out of her prison. She sat on the stairs, her head in her hands. All she could do is wait.

Wait for what, she didn't know. Wait for Adam to go crazy and kill her? Wait for Jake to come and rescue her?

She thought about Matty. If she ever got out of here but couldn't make it home in time, Jake would surely take care of him. If no one was home when Matty got home from school, he knew enough to go next door to Kyle's, where Chrissy would watch him.

But what if she never got out of here alive? Who would

take care of Matty then? And who would take care of Jake?

She stood and turned around when the lock on the door at the top of the steps rattled. The door opened and Adam stood in the doorway. He looked at her a moment before heading down the steps, then stopped and waved her back.

She moved to the far wall, leaned back, and waited while he continued his slow plod to the basement floor.

He stopped a few feet from her, his shoulders slumped as he rocked back and forth on his heels. Annie waited for him to speak.

He moistened his lips, fiddling with a button on his shirt. "I think ..." His voice cracked. He cleared his throat and took a deep breath. "I think I just killed someone." He looked at Annie as if hoping for comfort, his eyes pleading with her.

She spoke softly. "Who'd you kill?"

"I ... I don't know for sure. I can't remember, but I know it in my heart, just like last time. A vague memory I know is true, but I have no idea who it was or any of the details." He wrung his hands.

She took a step toward him but he held up a hand to stop her. "You'd better not come near me." He closed his eyes a moment, squeezing them tight. Then he opened them and said, "It happens when I get agitated. When I think about how much my life sucks. Then the voices start and I lose it entirely."

"What did the voices say?" Annie asked.

His eyes narrowed at the thought. "They told me to kill you."

Annie took a sharp breath and a step backwards, her back now to the wall. Is that why he was here now? Had he listened to the voices?

A faint smile appeared on his lips. "Don't worry," he said. "I didn't listen to them. Sometimes they go away, and I think they only force me to do something that part of me already wants to do."

Annie felt a measure of relief and spoke carefully. "Part of you wanted to go and kill someone today?"

He shrugged. "I guess so."

"You don't know?"

"I'm trying to understand what goes on in my head and what causes me to do those crazy things." He shook his head and sighed. "I know there's no one in my head except me, but it's so real." His voice turned bitter. "You can't begin to understand what it's like."

Annie's studies had supplied her with a working knowledge of schizophrenia, but she realized knowing about it and experiencing it were two entirely different things. All the knowledge in the world couldn't bring her to understand Adam's pain.

But at the same time, he was a dangerous man. For the sake of everyone around him, he had to be contained, and ultimately, there was no scenario in which Adam Thorburn could come through this a winner.

She glanced toward the steps, wondering if she could make a dash for it before Adam could react and stop her. She decided against it. Even in his dejected state, he was still being cautious, and it wouldn't end well for her.

He straightened up, drew back his shoulders, and watched her closely while he said, "I want to kill myself. Will you help me?"

Annie's mouth widened and she shook her head adamantly. "Never."

"I didn't think you would. It was just a thought." He sighed deeply and looked away. "I don't have the strength to do it myself."

"That's not the answer, Adam."

"I tried already. Twice. Once upstairs with the gun, and once in the swamp. I tried to drown myself and it almost worked, but something stopped me."

"In the swamp?" Annie asked. "Is that where you've been for two days?"

"I like it there," he said. "It brings me peace, but now that Jake has discovered it, I can't go back."

Annie's breathing quickened. Jake was looking for her. Of course she had suspected as much, but he might be getting close.

"Where's Jake?" she asked cautiously.

He shrugged one shoulder. "I don't know. I hope he went away."

Annie doubted that. Jake would still be in the area, and though she knew he was a little reckless sometimes, she prayed he would be careful if he ever met up with Adam. And she had to believe he would find her. It was all she had to cling to.

She tried a different tactic. "Adam, maybe Jake and I could help you get away from here. Somewhere far away. That's what you said you wanted."

He laughed. "That's very kind of you, but I know you don't mean that. You know how dangerous I am, and it would be rather irresponsible of you to help me." He paused. "Nice try, though."

Annie shrugged. "Okay, I'll admit, it was a pathetic attempt, but there's one thing I know for certain. I don't wish you any harm and you don't wish me any harm. All I want is what's best for everyone."

He nodded. "I do, too. That's the problem with our situation. We don't see eye to eye on what's best for me." He gave a short laugh, maybe from self-pity, or perhaps from the irony of the situation. "I know what's right for everyone else. For me to go back to the swamp, jump in, and do it right this time."

"Think about your mother, Adam. Think about what it would do to her."

"I'm not so sure she cares. I've been a millstone around her neck ever since Dad died, and she might be just about fed up with taking care of me. Besides, she can't afford it. My father left a little money in an account after he died, but that's long gone."

Annie had no answer to that. It seemed unlikely a mother would abandon her child, but in the real world, it happened sometimes.

"Whether or not she cares," he continued. "It's still better for her if I wasn't around to cause her more headaches."

His eyes grew damp and he turned and paced the floor, his head down. He stopped at the wall, drew back a fist, and pounded the concrete. He howled in pain, emotional and physical, and stared at his wounded knuckles. There was fire in his eyes when he turned back to face Annie, and she shrank back against the wall.

She watched in horror as he reached behind his back, withdrew the pistol, and held it up, glaring at it. He turned the barrel slowly until it pointed directly at her. His hand trembled, his finger shook on the trigger, and she saw his mind in turmoil. She held her breath, not daring to breathe.

He dropped his head back suddenly, his palms over his ears, and screamed, "Leave me alone. Leave me alone. I won't do it."

Then he turned abruptly, dropped his weapon hand, and raced up the stairs two at a time. The door slammed shut behind him, the lock slid closed, and Annie slumped against the wall, able to breathe again.

CHAPTER 43

Thursday, 2:18 p.m.

JAKE'S PATIENCE looked like it was about to pay off.

He watched from his hiding place in a thick hedge as Virginia Thorburn walked purposefully down the driveway to the sidewalk. She carried a grocery bag in one hand, a handbag in the other. He looked at his watch. It was much too early for her to be heading to work, and nobody takes a stuffed grocery bag out of the house except to deliver something. Jake was pretty sure he knew what the occasion was.

She was going to see Adam.

She cast a quick glance at the unmarked car across the street, waved a hand their way, then stepped onto the sidewalk. She strolled away, casually swinging the bag as if out for an afternoon stroll.

Jake waited until she was fifty feet away before crawling out of the hedge. He walked up the sidewalk keeping pace with her, careful to keep one of the many trees that lined the street between them whenever possible. If Virginia happened to get the slightest glimpse of him, he would be recognized immediately. For Annie's sake, Jake couldn't let that happen.

She reached the end of the block, turned around slowly, and gazed his way. He pulled his head back behind a massive tree trunk and waited, daring to peer out a few seconds later.

She had turned at the intersection and was heading up the short street that led from Mill Street to Steel Road. In a moment, she disappeared from sight. Jake stepped out, jogged to the corner, and frowned. She was gone.

Then through his peripheral vision, off to his right, he saw the screen door at the side of the corner house snap shut. He dropped down. That had to be where she'd gone; it was the only way she could've vanished so quickly.

Was Adam hiding out in there?

Was Annie in there?

He was going to find out.

He surveyed the house. It looked uninhabited. There were no curtains on the windows, the grass was overgrown, and no lights were visible inside. It was the perfect hiding place, and totally unexpected.

He had visited the house earlier and no one had answered the door, but it was only one of several where no one was home and he hadn't given it a second thought.

Jake walked boldly to the porch, stepped up, and took a quick glimpse inside the small window in the door. He couldn't see clearly through the screen, and he craned his neck in both directions. The entranceway appeared to be empty.

He stepped off the porch and circled around to the back of the house. A door exited onto a small deck, a sliding glass door, probably leading to the kitchen. He eased across the wall of the house and moved onto the deck, choosing his steps carefully. The boards were rotting in places, and a wrong step would send a loud warning to anyone in the house.

Jake clung to the wall, inched toward the door, and stopped. He held his breath and peered around carefully.

He pulled back abruptly and let his breath out. Virginia sat at the kitchen table, facing his way. She might have seen him had her view not been blocked by a man who sat at the near end of the table, his back toward the door.

He didn't see the man's face, but it had to be Adam. Who else would be hanging around a deserted dwelling? Virginia wouldn't be making a friendly neighborhood visit to an empty house.

Now Jake had a choice to make. Should he go barging in, or wait for Virginia to leave? And what if one, or both of them, had a weapon? Normally he would dive right in, but he had to think of Annie. He wasn't sure whether or not she was there, but if so, he couldn't endanger her. One person, even a raging psychopath, would be easier to handle than two, especially if one of them was a mother who might do whatever it took to protect her son.

Jake made up his mind. He eased off the deck and moved across the lawn to the sidewalk. He stepped behind a tree where a cursory glance now and then would give him a view of the side and back doors at the same time.

He waited and watched.

Finally, the side door opened and Virginia stepped out. She waved a hand, strode to the sidewalk, and rounded the corner. She was heading home again, and Jake was raring to go.

He waited until she was safely out of sight and then moved to the door, opened the screen door as quietly as possible, and twisted the knob. The door was locked from the inside. He stood back and examined the frame. It didn't look so strong and wouldn't stand much chance against his wide shoulder and two hundred and ten pounds of muscle behind it.

Jake took a deep breath and lunged forward. The door complained but held. He shook his head, stepped back, and hit the door again. The frame splintered, the door sprung forward, and Jake caught his balance and dove into the house.

"Stand back."

Jake spun his head. The man at the table was Adam, no doubt, but now he stood in the entrance to the living room holding a pistol gripped in both hands, a maniacal look on his face.

Jake held out a hand, palm out. "You'd better put the gun down, Adam."

Adam shook his head. "Never."

"Is my wife here?"

"Who's your wife?"

"You know who she is. Her name's Annie." Jake raised his voice and bellowed, "Annie?"

"I'll shoot you," Adam said, his eyes wild, his hands shaking.

Jake looked at the trembling hands of the madman. Adam didn't look like he would be able to hit a moving target, but Jake wasn't going to take any chances. He tucked his hands into his pockets in an attempt to look like less of a threat.

"You can leave if you want," he said. "I only want my wife."

"Jake," a muffled voice called and Jake's heart jumped. It was Annie and she was okay. He looked toward the sound and saw a door, probably leading to the basement. He turned back to Adam, who looked frantically back and forth between the basement door and Jake.

"I didn't hurt her," Adam said.

"Thank you," Jake said, attempting to put the maniac at ease. "You're not a killer."

Adam cocked his head and the gun wavered, dropping a couple of inches. Jake dove forward, hitting Adam with a perfect sliding tackle. The gun flew through the air and Adam went down, the breath knocked out of him. The gun bounced on the carpet and lay out of Adam's reach, no longer a threat.

The fugitive clawed at Jake with both hands in vain. Jake grabbed Adam's wrists and climbed to his feet, pulling his captive with him, then wrenched the man's arms behind his back and held him firmly in one massive fist.

"You're under arrest."

Adam dropped his head, his rage expended, and remained still.

Jake half-dragged Adam toward the basement door, slid the lock back with his free hand, and pulled the door open. He grinned at Annie as she stepped into the room.

She looked up into his warm brown eyes, and whispered, "I've never been so happy to see you."

Adam twisted his head around and looked at Annie with moist eyes. He spoke in a low, pleading voice. "Make sure you tell them I didn't hurt you."

Jake couldn't understand the compassion on Annie's face as she looked at the captive with a faint smile and said, "You didn't harm me."

She let go of Jake, went to the kitchen, and glanced around. Her handbag lay on the counter, still intact. She dug inside and removed her cell phone. It was undamaged, with the GPS turned off.

"We'd better call the police now," Jake said.

CHAPTER 44

Thursday, 3:12 p.m.

HANK WAS THRILLED when he heard about the arrest of Adam Thorburn. He didn't care who got the credit. He was only thankful another vicious killer had been apprehended.

When the precinct doors opened and Adam was brought in, Hank picked up the evidence folder from his desk and pushed back his chair. He stood to his feet, beckoned to King, and strolled across the precinct. The prisoner's head was down, his shoulders slumped, his hands cuffed securely behind his back as two officers prodded him across the floor.

Jake and Annie came behind the procession, a wide grin appearing on Jake's face when Hank approached.

Hank shook Jake's hand and gave Annie a sideways hug. "Congratulations, guys."

"Couldn't have done it without you, Hank," Jake said. "As far as I'm concerned, it's your arrest."

Annie agreed. "It's your case—your arrest."

Detective King wandered over, his hands stuffed in his pockets, and watched without a word as Adam was led down a hallway away from the room. The suspect would be taken to Interview Room One and Hank looked forward to interrogating him.

Hank turned to Jake. "You guys are welcome to watch the interview. We owe you that much." He looked at King. "You ready?"

King shrugged. "Ready as I'll ever be."

Hank led the way across the floor, down the hallway, and opened a door. He motioned for the Lincolns to enter the room. From there, they could listen to the interview and watch it through a one-way mirror.

He closed the door and opened the next one, and King followed him inside. Adam Thorburn sat on the far side of a small metal table, his head down, his hands cuffed to a secure bar on the tabletop. His eyes turned upward as Hank pulled back a chair, tossed the folder onto the table, and sat down.

King stood and leaned against the wall of the bare room and observed the prisoner. The small room was bleak, with a camera in the corner to record the interview. The one-way mirror was behind Hank.

Adam Thorburn raised his head and looked cautiously at Hank, fear in his eyes, the cufflinks rattling as he wrung his hands.

Hank opened the folder, leafed blankly through the pages,

then leaned forward. "You're going to be charged with two counts of murder, possibly kidnapping, unlawful possession of a firearm, and who knows what else."

Adam nodded and remained silent.

"Tell me about the murder of Nina White," Hank said.

Adam breathed rapidly, his body shaking. "I … I don't remember." He paused. "I ran over her with a car."

King rested his hands on the edge of the desk and leaned in. "Why?"

Adam looked up at King and shook his head. "I … I don't know."

"Were you in love with her?"

Adam's brow tightened. "No. Of course not. She was good to me, that's all."

"Then why'd you kill her?" King demanded.

Adam shrugged and rubbed his hand together to control the trembling.

"What about Raymond Ronson?" Hank asked. "Why'd you kill him?"

Adam shrugged again. "I … I don't know why. Sometimes I can't help myself. I hear voices telling me to do things, and sometimes I don't remember doing them."

King raised his voice. "So you're going to plead temporary insanity. Is that your game?"

"I'm not insane," Adam said to King, and looked at Hank. "I have schizophrenia."

"And you're a psychopath," King added, straightening his back. "And a sociopath."

Adam shook uncontrollably. He closed his eyes, took a

deep breath, and let it out slowly. When he opened his eyes, he looked fearfully at Hank. "Are you going to lock me up?"

King laughed out loud. "That's usually what we do with killers. We lock them up forever."

Hank frowned up at King. Hank wanted the young man to relax and tell them what they needed to know, but King wasn't helping with his fear-mongering.

"Tell me about Raymond Ronson," Hank asked, his voice taking on a softer tone.

Adam took a couple of breaths. "Everybody at school knew Mr. Ronson. He liked to talk to the kids and get to know us. He was real friendly."

Hank leaned in, resting his arms on the table. "So why'd you kill him after all these years?"

Adam hung his head, his voice barely low enough to hear. "I don't know."

"What about the third one? The one you told Annie about on the phone?"

Adam raised his head. "I barely remember that one. Some of it came back to me. I remember blood and a knife."

"Who was the victim, Adam?"

"I ... I don't know. I felt a lot of hatred."

"Who do you hate, Adam?"

Adam looked bewildered. "I don't hate anyone."

"What about the boys who used to bully you at school?"

Adam nodded slowly. "Yeah, I guess I hate them. Sometimes."

"Did you kill one of them, Adam?"

Adam stared blankly at Hank, then his eyes widened and he took a sharp breath. "Maybe."

"Think," King shouted, leaning on the desk.

Hank looked at the impatient cop. "You're not helping. You're only agitating him."

King huffed and leaned back against the wall.

Hank touched Adam's hand. "Was it one of the bullies?"

Adam nodded once, stopped to think, then nodded again. "Yes, it was." His eyes filled with dread at the thought. "I think I remember now."

"Do you remember his name?"

The prisoner stared at the ceiling a moment then closed his eyes. Then his eyes popped open and he stared at Hank. "It was Patton. His name's Paul Patton." He blinked rapidly. "It was at the grocery store where I work. He's a stockboy and I knew him from school." He dropped his head into his hands and moaned.

Hank sat back. It appeared they were finally getting somewhere. He glanced at King, removed a pen from his jacket, and wrote down the name.

"What did you do with the body?"

Adam looked up, tears in his eyes. "I ... I put him in the dumpster behind the store."

That's why the body had never been found. It was probably long gone, perhaps buried under a mountain of trash in a landfill somewhere.

Adam breathed rapidly, erratically, the tears now escaping from his eyes. He tried to speak, his body shivering, the cuffs rattling as he shook. Through sobs, he managed to say, "There ... there's another one."

"Another victim?" Hank asked.

Adam nodded furiously, tears dripping off his chin. He dropped his head and wiped them away with a cuffed hand. "I can remember some of it now, too. It happened this morning."

"Tell me about it." Hank was shocked, but he kept his voice soft, encouraging the young man to continue.

"Richdale Pizza."

Hank waited until Adam recovered enough to continue.

"Ira Toddle."

"Was he a bully too?"

"Yes," Adam whispered. "He was."

Hank wrote the name down before asking, "He worked at Richdale Pizza?"

Adam nodded.

"Where did you kill him?"

Adam could barely speak. "Behind the store. I ... I shot him. In the face."

"Where's the body?"

"I hid it behind a parked car."

Hank spoke in a low voice. "Were there any more, Adam?"

Adam shook his head. "That's all. I'm pretty sure." He raised his eyes toward Hank, pleading, "Please help me."

"We'll get you some help." Hank closed the folder, picked it up, then looked over at King. "That's enough for now. We'd better check out these bodies and continue from there."

King nodded, bounced off the wall, opened the door, and Hank followed him out. King wandered back to the precinct while Hank stepped into the next room.

Jake and Annie turned toward him as he entered. Hank glanced at Annie. Her eyes were moist, but he said nothing about it and turned to Jake.

"He's a pretty messed-up guy," Hank said. He glanced through the glass where Adam still shook, his head in his hands. The man's sobs came through the speaker. Hank turned back to Annie. "Thanks for your help on this one. Diego will be extremely pleased."

"I'm just happy it's wrapped up," Annie said, her voice shaking.

Jake turned to Annie. "Shall we go?"

Annie nodded and followed Jake from the room. Jake turned back, leaned through the doorway, and grinned at Hank. "I'll let you tell Teddy White the news," he said, then closed the door.

Hank watched the prisoner a few moments longer before going back to his desk. He was disturbed about the news of a fourth victim, but relieved it was finally over.

CHAPTER 45

Thursday, 3:52 p.m.

ANNIE SAT QUIETLY in the passenger seat as Jake pulled the Firebird out of the precinct parking lot. Adam would finally get the help he so desperately needed, but his life was about to undergo a drastic change.

His mother would be brought in for questioning before long, and when she heard the news of Adam's arrest, she would be devastated. She had protected him through it all, but she'd broken the law in doing so.

Annie's heart ached for everyone concerned, and other than her drinking buddy next door, Virginia Thorburn had no one to talk to.

She turned to face Jake. "I want to drop by and see Mrs. Thorburn."

Jake glanced over and raised an eyebrow. "It's over, honey."

"It's not over for everyone. It's just starting."

"I'm not sure if she wants to see me," Jake said. "I didn't get a very warm reception last time."

"She's under a lot of stress," Annie said. "Besides, I have a few things I'd like to talk to her about. She's going to be in a lot of trouble once the police bring her in and I don't think she realizes it. I want to get some facts straight before she gets a lawyer and clams up."

Jake gave a soft sigh, pulled to the side of the street, and made a U-turn. "You'd better call Chrissy."

Annie took out her phone, called her friend and told her they would be awhile yet, asking if she would watch Matty a little longer. Chrissy informed her it was no problem and Annie hung up the phone.

In a few minutes, they turned onto Mill Street and drove toward the Thorburn residence. The police car that had sat across the road from the house was now gone. The officers hiding in the garage were likely relieved as well and would move on to the next task.

Jake pulled the Firebird to the side of the street in front of the house. They stepped out, went to the side door, and opened the screen. Jake knocked on the inner door and waited. After a few moments, he knocked again.

"I don't think she's home right now," he said.

Annie peered through the window in the door. "She might've gone to work."

"It's a little early for that," Jake said, looking at his watch.

Annie stepped off the porch. "Maybe we can come back later."

Jake shrugged and followed Annie out to the street. Annie glanced down the sidewalk. A woman was walking toward them from some distance away, carrying a large handbag, and it looked like Mrs. Thorburn. "I think that's her," Annie said, pointing. "I wonder if she knows about Adam yet."

Jake squinted up the sidewalk. "That's her," he said, leaning against a tree. He pointed a thumb over his shoulder. "And I'm pretty sure if she'd gone to see Adam, she'd still be there wondering why the place is filled with cops. Besides, she's coming from the wrong direction. I don't think she knows yet."

"She'll find out soon enough," Annie said. She walked a few feet toward the woman, waved a hand, and waited. "We wanted to see how you're doing," Annie said, when the woman drew closer.

Virginia frowned at Jake and then gave Annie a faint smile. "I'm doing fine."

"May we come in a minute?"

The woman hesitated, adjusted the handbag on her shoulder, then motioned toward the house. "I can spare a few minutes, but I need to get ready for work soon." She turned and walked up the driveway.

Annie and Jake followed the woman to the house. Virginia dug her key from her handbag, unlocked the door, and swung it open. They stepped inside and the woman motioned for them to have a seat at the dining room table.

"Do you want anything? Coffee? Beer?" she asked.

Jake looked at Annie. "I'll have a coffee."

"Coffee, thanks," Annie said.

The Lincolns sat at the table while the woman went to the kitchen. Annie glanced around at the assortment of items on the table. It was no tidier than last time and she wondered if the woman ever did any cleaning at all. An ashtray bulging with butts sat at the end of the table—Virginia's favorite spot.

"I hope the coffee's drinkable," Jake whispered. He had noticed the mess too. He pushed back a plate that sat in front of him and brushed away some bread crumbs.

"Don't be rude," Annie said.

Jake chuckled. "She didn't hear me."

Virginia came in the room a moment later carrying a cup in one hand and juggling two in the other. She set them on the table and pushed one toward each of them. "I hope you like cream and sugar," she said.

"It's perfect," Annie said, taking a sip. Jake agreed.

Mrs. Thorburn sat down in her spot, pulled a cigarette from a pack, and used the tip of it to rearrange the butts in the ashtray to make room for more. She lit it, closed her eyes and took a deep drag, blowing the smoke into the air above Annie's head.

"What did you want to talk about?" she asked.

"About Adam," Annie answered. She hesitated and studied Virginia's face. "Do you know he's been arrested?"

Virginia Thorburn stopped halfway through another drag of her cigarette, her eyes bulging. Her mouth dropped open and the smoke worked its own way out. She waved it away with a hand and leaned in, speechless, her mouth still open.

"Just an hour or so ago," Jake said. "Annie wanted to make sure you're okay."

The woman dropped her head into her hands, the cigarette coming dangerously close to singeing her hair. "Oh, no," she moaned, then raised her head and asked quickly, "Is he all right?"

"He's fine," Annie said. "He's at the police station."

Virginia looked fearful. "He's going to need a lawyer but I can't afford it."

"They'll find him a legal aid lawyer, a public defender," Jake said.

Annie knew the woman had talked to her son but didn't know if she was aware of the last two murders. She didn't want to bring them up right now; Virginia would find out soon enough. She looked closely at the distraught woman and said, "His memory is hazy on the murders of Nina White and Raymond Ronson. He can't remember any of the details." She hesitated. "Did he tell you anything at all about them?"

Virginia shook her head. "Last time I talked to him he didn't remember anything at all."

"He told me he was fond of both of them," Annie said. "That's what makes it so perplexing."

"He didn't know what he was doing," Virginia said, tears in her eyes. "Maybe that's why he put the roses in their mouths, a symbol of some kind to show he cared about them."

Annie glanced at Jake as he coughed, choking on a swig of coffee. She turned back to Mrs. Thorburn. "We thought perhaps he had a crush on Nina White at one time. Did he ever mention that?"

Virginia shook her head. "Not to me."

Jake stood. "I think I'll get a little more cream in my coffee if you don't mind." He picked up his cup and wandered toward the kitchen.

Annie continued, "The police are going to want to talk to you soon."

Virginia nodded her head, her voice weak. "I know." She looked at Annie, her eyes pleading. "But I was only trying to help my son."

"I realize that," Annie said. "I'm sure they'll take that into consideration."

Jake returned, put his coffee cup on the table and sat, leaning toward the woman. "Mrs. Thorburn," he asked, "how did you know about the roses in the mouths of the victims? The police didn't release that information."

Virginia's eyes widened and she stared at Jake. "I ... I. Adam must've told me."

"Adam doesn't remember any of the details," Jake said flatly, then raised his voice. "What're you not telling us?" He stood and dropped his arms on the table, leaning in closer. "Why does Adam not remember the first two murders but you know all about them?"

Annie looked curiously at her husband. She wasn't sure what he was up to, but he had a good point about the roses and the woman's knowledge of the murders.

Virginia didn't answer Jake's questions. She looked frantically back and forth between Jake and Annie.

"You claim to be such a caring mother," Jake continued. "And yet you don't want your son to get the help he needs.

That made me very suspicious, but now I know for sure." He narrowed his eyes. "Virginia Thorburn," he said, his voice taking on an accusing tone, "did you kill Nina White and Raymond Ronson and frame your son?"

The woman gasped and froze, staring at Jake. Then she pushed back her chair and stumbled into the kitchen.

Annie stared bug-eyed, the realization hitting her. She sprang after the woman, then stopped short when Virginia stepped from the kitchen, a grim look on her face and a shiny new pistol gripped in one hand.

"You just couldn't leave it alone," she said. "You couldn't mind your own business and now you leave me no choice."

Jake still sat at the table. Annie stepped backwards and dropped into her chair as Virginia moved to a phone on the wall, picked up the receiver, and dialed a number.

"You'd better get over here," the woman said into the phone. "We have a big problem."

CHAPTER 46

Thursday, 4:21 p.m.

HANK HAD A STACK of paperwork to do, a lot of loose ends to tie up, and a long list of questions he needed answered before he could close the case and take a much-needed rest.

Adam Thorburn had been placed in a holding cell and put on suicide watch. He was given a change of clothes, his old ones taken to the lab for forensic experts to examine. Traces of gunshot residue, blood spatter, and anything found in his pockets would be examined and documented.

The suspected murder weapon found at the old Cochran house where Adam had hidden out was also in the lab, and it would be inspected as well. CSI was still at the scene where they would go over the dwelling thoroughly. Their report would be forthcoming, but Hank didn't expect it would shed any further light on the investigation. Everything was pretty cut and dried.

He'd sent King out with a handful of officers to locate the bodies of the two latest victims Adam had mentioned. They'd be gone awhile, and Hank wanted to get as much work as possible done on the case before they returned.

Following the interview of Adam Thorburn, the Lincolns had left the precinct without giving their statements. They had to get home to Matty. Hank planned to drop by their place later and get the rest of the details, but for now, he was satisfied with the information he'd obtained from them.

And now, he wanted to request a warrant for the arrest of Virginia Thorburn. He had sufficient factual information to establish probable cause she'd committed a crime, and a written affidavit to a judge would be all that was necessary. She would be brought in, questioned at length, and charged with harboring a fugitive. It would then be up to the crown whether or not they wanted to pursue those charges, but Hank had to do his job.

He thumbed through a stack of paperwork on the edge of his desk, removed the folder on Virginia Thorburn, and leafed through it. As he copied the pertinent information to the arrest warrant, something caught his eye. Something didn't add up that he never noticed before.

He decided to dig a little deeper and he turned to his computer, searching through a variety of databases. From what he could find through birth, death, and marriage records, Virginia and Adam's father, Mason Thorburn, had been married eight years ago. Virginia was Adam's stepmother, not his mother.

Adam's birth mother had died when he was an infant, and Virginia was the only mother he'd ever known. That must be why Adam always referred to her as his mother. And when Mason had died almost a year ago, she'd been the only family he had left.

It appeared the death of Adam's father might've been the turning point in his life. That's when he began to worsen, his mental illness producing new and frightful symptoms, ultimately leading to murder.

Hank's phone rang and he answered it. It was Rod Jameson calling from the forensic lab. "Hank," Jameson said. "We went over Thorburn's clothes as well as the weapon. Normally, we would document everything and get it to you as soon as possible, but I wanted to give you a heads-up on our findings—or should I say, our lack thereof."

"What did you come up with, Rod?" Hank asked.

"We went over the subject's clothing thoroughly and there were no traces of blood or gunshot residue on any of the articles or on his shoes."

"He probably changed his clothes," Hank said. "Perhaps they'll find his other clothing at the Cochran house."

"I've been in touch with them," Rod said. "They didn't find anything. He could've thrown them out somewhere. That's always a possibility, but I wanted to fill you in."

"Okay, thanks, Rod. Appreciate it."

"That's not all."

"I'm listening," Hank said.

"We checked the pistol removed from the Cochran house and I believe there's no mistake. It's brand new and appears never to have been fired. I can't tell a hundred per cent, because as you know, they test fire it at the factory and then clean it up. But if it was fired recently, Thorburn did a good job of cleaning it. There's no residue on it at all." Jameson paused and took a breath. "And the chamber is completely full."

Hank frowned. Jameson had supplied him with some interesting information, but until the body of the last victim was located, there was no solid evidence showing the gun in question was the one used in the shooting.

"Thanks for the info, Rod. Anything else?"

"That's it for now. I'll let you know if we find anything I think you should know about. It's going to take awhile to process the scene."

Hank thanked him again, hung up thoughtfully, and went back to the paperwork.

He looked up a few moments later when Detective King came into the precinct and ducked into Diego's office. He was surprised King was back so soon and hoped they had located the bodies of the two victims.

Hank waited patiently until King left Diego's office, then frowned when the cop went into the break room. Hank sat back in his chair, crossed his arms, and waited.

Two minutes later, King appeared again, a faint smile on his face as he approached Hank. He dropped into the guest chair and leaned back, stretching out his legs. King took a slug of his coffee, sat the cup carefully on the edge of Hank's desk, and leaned back again, folding his arms.

Hank looked at King and frowned impatiently. "So, what's going on? Did you find the bodies?"

King shook his head. "We never found any bodies, Hank."

"No bodies? Then why're you back here so soon?"

King uncrossed his arms and leaned forward. "Because Paul Patton and Ira Toddle are both alive and doing well."

CHAPTER 47

Thursday, 5:17 p.m.

JAKE SAT SIDEWAYS, one elbow on the table, and looked over at Annie. His wife was turned in her chair, watching Virginia Thorburn hold the pistol firmly in front of her, its barrel toward them.

The woman didn't look any more of an expert with a gun than her son, but at least Virginia held the weapon steady as she stared coldly down the sights toward Annie.

Annie looked back at her and spoke in a calm voice. "Mrs. Thorburn, you might as well give up now. The police will be here to arrest you soon, and you're going to make things worse for yourself."

Virginia Thorburn glanced toward the door and didn't answer.

Jake spoke. "You did a brilliant job, Virginia. You had everything figured out perfectly, but you blew it."

The woman glared at Jake.

"Before you kill us, tell me the reason for all this," he said. "What's in it for you?"

Virginia moved half a step closer, aiming the gun toward Jake, her eyes narrowing. "Adam's a burden and a complete waste of my time. He's twenty-one years old and still hanging around for me to take care of." Her lips tightened and she shook her head. "I'm not about to babysit him the rest of his miserable life."

"And so all this was your plan to get rid of him?" Annie asked. "Frame him for two murders and get him thrown in prison and out of your hair?"

"I expected the kid would get shot," Virginia said. "That's why I gave him the gun. I hoped he would either get killed by the police or kill himself."

"That's the best idea you could come up with?" Annie said. "Couldn't you just tell him to leave?"

Virginia smiled. "It goes a little deeper than that. My dear dead husband had quite a chunk of change handed to him when his mother died. Unfortunately, except for a small amount, the idiot put it in a trust account to cover Adam's ongoing care. My husband named me as executor if anything happened to him, but I couldn't get at it for my own use." She let out a guttural chuckle. "That is, unless something happened to Adam."

"And then we threw a monkey wrench into your plans," Jake said.

She shrugged a shoulder. "It doesn't matter. You two are an annoyance, but once we get rid of you, the plan will continue."

"We?" Jake asked.

Virginia laughed. "I had a little help."

Tires crackled on gravel and Jake glanced toward the window as a car pulled into the driveway. It moved forward out of his view, the engine died, and a car door slammed.

Virginia moved toward the door, swung it open, and stood back, her eyes still on her captives.

The screen door opened and a man stepped into the room, a grim look on his face. Jake's eyes bulged. It was Dr. Zalora.

The doctor glared at Jake, then at Annie, a deep frown on his face. He looked at Virginia, perplexed. "What happened?" he asked.

Virginia pointed an accusing finger. "They figured it out."

Jake glared at Dr. Zalora. Why was he involved in this, and what did he hope to gain? As if in answer, the doctor touched Virginia on the arm and spoke in a soothing voice. "It's not too late, darling. We can easily get rid of them."

Jake and Annie exchanged a glance. It was finally making some sense. Virginia and the doctor were having an affair, and they had teamed up to dispose of Adam and gain control of his trust fund.

The doctor glared at Jake with cold eyes then turned to Virginia and held out his hand. "I'll take the gun." He laughed and winked at her. "You killed two. I'll kill the next two."

Virginia passed the gun to Zalora. The doctor wrapped his

hand around the butt, placing his finger firmly on the trigger. He looked at Jake. "I prefer not to do it here, but if you try anything stupid, I'll shoot both of you here and now." He sighed. "It'll make more of a mess that way, but the end result will be the same."

"If you'll permit me one question," Annie said, looking at Virginia, "how could you have killed Nina White? Your neighbor, Mabel, said you were with her."

Virginia chuckled. "I was with her all right—until she passed out." She laughed. "That woman never could hold her booze, and she never knew I left long enough to take care of a little business."

"But why kill Nina White and Raymond Ronson? They were two people Adam liked."

The woman shrugged. "No particular reason. It had to be someone Adam knew, and those were the only two he ever talked about. He unknowingly led me right to them."

"Why'd you kill two?" Jake asked. "Wasn't one enough?"

"It should've been, but the police failed to track Adam to the swamp and shoot him down. I had to give them another reason to get serious about finding him."

"But you're the one who warned him to run," Annie said. "Why?"

"Because I didn't want him caught." She raised her voice and spoke through gritted teeth. "I wanted him dead."

"And so you killed two innocent people."

She gave an evil chuckle. "It's their own fault for being so friendly with a psychopath like Adam."

"The only thing is, he's not the psychopath here," Jake said. "You are."

Dr. Zalora's eyes gleamed. "That's not what the police think. They're convinced he's stark raving mad, thanks to my professional opinion."

Virginia laughed. "And a few drugs."

Annie leaned in and seemed about to leap forward, but Zalora waved the gun and glared darkly. "Sit down."

Annie sat back and crossed her arms. "So Adam's not a sociopath?"

Dr. Zalora glanced at Virginia, a wicked twinkle in his eye, then he laughed long and loud. When his face finally sobered, he said, "He's only as crazy as the drugs made him. You'd be surprised what a mix of certain medications can do to a person."

Jake jumped to his feet. "So, you drugged him and that made him crazy enough to kill two other people?"

Zalora smiled and sighted down the barrel toward Jake. "That was a bonus. The icing on the cake, you might say. I never expected that, and it was a pleasant surprise." His voice took on a menacing tone. "Now sit down."

Jake dropped back into the chair. "And the purpose of the roses in the victim's mouths?"

Virginia shrugged. "Just a little more evidence against Adam."

"That's enough talk," Dr. Zalora said. "We have to get this finished."

"I agree with you," Jake said. "It's time to get this cleaned up. I need to go home for a little nap."

Dr. Zalora frowned. "You'll get your nap. Both of you. For the rest of eternity."

Jake stood and reached into his shirt pocket. "I recorded everything," he said, pulling out a small recorder. He looked at it. "It's amazing how well this thing picks up conversations."

Dr. Zalora moved in a step and glared. "Too bad you won't be able to use it." He held out a hand. "Give it to me."

Jake dropped the recorder back into his pocket and took a step forward, now only five feet from the deadly weapon pointed toward his head.

Annie looked at Jake with alarm. "Jake, sit down."

"You'd better listen to your wife," Zalora said.

Jake stretched out an arm and spoke calmly. "Give me the gun."

"Stay back," Zalora shouted, his finger tightening on the trigger.

Annie screamed. "Jake. Sit down!"

Jake kept his hand out and took another step.

Dr. Zalora growled and squeezed the trigger.

The gun went click, click.

Jake moved in, grabbed the pistol, and with one punch, he knocked Dr. Zalora to the floor. Virginia gasped and moved back against the wall, staring down at her accomplice, her mouth and eyes wide.

The doctor lay stunned a moment, then groaned and shook his head to clear his senses. He looked up at Virginia in confusion.

Annie was unable to speak, her mouth gaping open as she watched.

Jake reached a hand into the pocket of his pants, then

removed his fist and opened it, palm up. "Are you looking for these?"

Virginia's expression didn't change from one of shock as she stared at the fistful of ammunition in the palm of Jake's hand. "How? What?"

Jake shrugged. "Simple. After I realized you were the killer, I went to the kitchen pretending to get some more cream in my coffee. I did a quick search, checked a couple of drawers, finally found the gun in your handbag, and removed the ammunition." He laughed. "Oh, I could've nabbed you right there, but I wanted your confession first." He tapped his shirt pocket and smiled. "And now I have it."

Virginia watched helplessly as Jake loaded the gun, sat down, and trained the weapon their way.

Jake chuckled. "I'm having a great day. How about you?"

Annie was finally able to speak, so she dug out her cell phone and dialed 9-1-1.

EPILOGUE

DAY 5 - Friday, 2:25 p.m.

ANNIE RELAXED in the living room of their modest house, curled up in her favorite chair, trying to catch up on some of her studies. Jake had taken the day off as well and had parked the Firebird in the sun, washing and polishing it to a dazzling shine.

Annie found it hard to concentrate on her reading, and she tucked the bookmark into her manual on police procedure and set it on the stand beside her chair.

She glanced out the front window. Hank had called a little earlier and said he was going to drop by to get their statements regarding the capture of the killers. She eagerly waited to see what he had to say about his interview with

Virginia Thorburn and Dr. Zalora, but more than that, she was concerned about Adam.

The young man had been subjected to a devious and heartbreaking plot, and whether or not he would be prosecuted for kidnapping, he faced some hard times.

Annie stood and moved closer to the window when Hank pulled his car in behind the Firebird. The cop got out, spoke briefly to Jake, and exchanged a laugh with him as the two guys headed for the house.

The pair were still chuckling about something when the front door opened and they stepped inside. Annie went over and leaned against the doorway between the living room and lobby. "What's so funny?"

Hank looked at her and grinned. "Hi, Annie. Jake was telling me about the little trick he pulled with the ammunition."

"Yeah, it was a barrel of laughs," Annie said dryly. She motioned toward the front room. "Come on in, Hank."

Annie went back to her chair and snuggled up while Jake and Hank sat on opposite ends of the couch. Hank set his briefcase between them and laid his arm along the back. "It's been a busy day. I'll go back to the precinct a little later and finish up, but for now, I'm taking a break. I'm on official police business anyway. I need to get your statements."

"Did you listen to the recording?" Jake asked.

Hank nodded. "It was muffled in a few places, but overall, we could make out everything that was said. Callaway said he could clean it up, and it's going to go a long way toward building our case against the two of them."

Jake chuckled. "That was an idea I got from Annie on our last big case."

Hank winked at Annie. "You're teaching him well."

"He has the occasional good idea," Annie said with a smile.

Jake gave a mock laugh and changed the subject. "Tell us about the interview with the two scumbags, Hank."

"The interviews weren't much of a challenge. Once we split them up and confronted them with the evidence and your recording, it didn't take much prodding to get the rest of the details. Especially from Virginia Thorburn. She tried to blame it all on the doctor at first, but soon broke down and spilled everything."

"What about the interview with Dr. Zalora?" Annie asked.

"Zalora got a lawyer immediately and tried to cut a deal. Claimed Virginia was the instigator and responsible for both murders. Which might be true, but it doesn't matter. He was totally complaisant with the whole thing. So we didn't budge. There was no need to make any kind of deal with him, especially since Virginia was so forthcoming."

"I'm curious about the name, "Adam Thor," written in blood at Nina White's murder," Jake said. "Was that done by Nina, or Virginia?"

Hank chuckled. "I think Virginia has watched too many horror movies. She was the one who wrote it, trying to lead us to Adam."

"So Virginia convinced Adam he was responsible, and he believed it because of his blackout spells."

"Exactly," Hank said. "And when Adam ran, it made him appear guilty."

"What about all the evidence against Adam?" Annie asked.

"She manufactured a lot of evidence against him at both scenes. It led us straight to Adam, but it was all circumstantial. Like the size eleven shoe prints at the Ronson murder. The prints were from Adam's shoes, but she wore them at the time."

"I'm concerned about Adam," Annie said. "What caused him to have so many blackouts and hallucinations?"

"Along with his regular antipsychotic medication to treat his schizophrenia, the doctor tried a variety of combinations before finally adding ketamine to the mix. It has anesthetic properties and can cause confusion and a lot of other problems if taken improperly. The plan was to make Adam violent and delusional so he could easily be blamed."

"And the whole thing was concocted to get rid of him?" Jake asked.

"It actually started off simply. Kill one person, frame Adam, and get rid of him. But it soon escalated out of control and they had to see it through. There was too much money at stake. Well over a million dollars."

"So after finding the right mix of drugs, they thought they had the perfect crime," Jake said.

"Exactly. Adam trusted the doctor and his stepmother, and it almost destroyed him. His hallucinations were increasing to the point where he often didn't know reality from delusion. He was convinced he killed four people. And since the last two took place only in his mind, he could remember them. Or thought he did."

"Hank, why were you not aware of the trust fund?" Jake asked.

"The fund, with strict limitations, had been set up in Virginia Thorburn's name, and she wasn't under any suspicion. To dig that deeply into her financial records would have required a warrant. A warrant we would have been unable to obtain without any real evidence against her."

Annie leaned forward. "What'll happen to Adam?"

"He's in the hospital right now. They've done blood tests to find out exactly what's in his system. He's being watched, more for his own protection than anything else. The police psychologist talked with him extensively, and he's of the opinion that not only will Adam recover, but his schizophrenia can be totally controlled."

"That's good news," Annie said. "But how is he emotionally?"

Hank shrugged. "He was devastated when he found out the truth, naturally. It's not easy to find out you've been betrayed by two people you trusted. And I dropped in to see him this morning. He can't seem to wrap his head around the fact he's going to be fine. He's on an emotional roller coaster, that's for sure, but he's in a much better mood now. Though he's confused about one thing."

"What's that?" Jake asked.

Hank laughed. "He doesn't understand why everyone is being so kind to him."

Annie smiled. "That young man is going to need a lot of love. He's been through so much."

Hank nodded. "He's going to get it, I'll bet. He's actually a likeable guy. With some counseling and a lot of emotional support, I'm betting he'll recover completely."

"What about criminal charges?" Jake asked. "I realize he broke the law, but I hope you're not going to lock him up."

Hank looked at Annie. "I assume you're not going to pursue kidnapping charges against him?"

"Not a chance."

Hank shrugged. "The only other thing is illegal possession of a firearm. I'm thankful he didn't hurt anyone. He didn't even fire it, and given the circumstances, I'm sure the crown won't prosecute."

"They won't," Annie said. "Once all this hits the press, the crown wouldn't take a chance on it. It would only make them look bad."

"Adam asked about you two," Hank said. "Even with all his problems, he felt concerned, especially about you, Annie. He wanted to know if you were okay."

"He'll find out this afternoon," Annie said. "I've got a big hug for him, and I plan on delivering it personally."

Jake grinned. "I think I'll go with her. I'd like to get to know the new Adam Thorburn."

"If you don't mind," Hank said. "I just might join you."

###

Made in the USA
Middletown, DE
13 December 2015